THE PUCK STOPS HERE

PHILIP STEPHENS

ISBN 978-1-956001-07-5 (paperback)
ISBN 978-1-956001-08-2 (eBook)

Printed in the United States of America

CHAPTER ONE

John and his brother Pete, lived in a neighborhood in Brooklyn with lots of kids around their same age. The area In Brooklyn was called Flatbush as Flatbush Avenue ran through the middle of the area. Pete was 18 months younger than John but the better athlete of the two. They played lots of street games as youngsters like stickball, ring-a-leaveo, johnny on a pony, triangle, off the wall, etc. Stickball was great because it helped the boys with really good hand to eye coordination that served them well in playing baseball. John belonged to a Social Athletic Club called the Senecas. The Senecas were an Indian tribe that lived in Upstate New York for hundreds of years. All of the Senecas wore green satin jackets with the name Senecas on the back and their first name on the front. The Senecas played all three major sports; basketball, baseball and football. They played in a league sponsored by the American Legion. John played 3rd base and was a very good fielder but not so much a good hitter. In basketball John played center as he was the tallest player on the team. He was a good rebounder and defender but not much of a scorer. When John was on the perimeter he would shoot a pretty good set shot which was a two handed shot. One of the players ended up as an Umpire in Major League Baseball. One of the football players ended up at the US Military Academy at West Point as a pretty good tailback.

John did excel playing football used as a wide receiver. He had some bad luck playing football. One year he broke his foot going up for a pass and landed awkwardly on the side of his foot. The next year he broke his leg and the ambulance took him to a local hospital. He was in a great deal of pain. When John's Mom got to the hospital, she noticed that in the bed next to John was a gun shot victim so she called a private ambulance service and took him to a private hospital. John was in a cast for several months and was given an elevator pass in school because he could not climb the stairs. The girls thought John was a hero and he played it for all it was worth. He did recover in time for the baseball season. Although John loved playing the three major sports, his favorite was roller hockey. They played roller hockey in the street using a big orange crate as the goal. Every time a car went by they had to stop the game. Got a bit dangerous from time to time. John would have loved to play Ice Hockey but the equipment was too expensive and there was hardly any place to play.

Pete was terrific baseball player. He was a good hitter and was an All-star 2nd baseman in High School. He also played Cornerback in Football in High School. Both boys did like watching Ice Hockey as kids. On Sunday when the New York Rangers were in town they played as part of a triple header at Madison Square Garden. The boys took the subway to 49th street station and walked to the Garden. They saw three games. The first was between two semi-pro teams. The second was the New York Rovers a farm team of the Rangers. The third game was the New York Rangers led by their goalie Dave Kerr and they won the Stanley Cup in 1940-1941

CHAPTER TWO

John fancied himself as a track star in high school in his first two years. He wanted to run the 100, 220 and 440 but he found out that he was not very competitive at those distances. The African American kids were the best at short distances. He did save up to buy spikes and sometimes he would take them to bed with him Today a kid could have his muscle fibers biopsyied to see whether he could run short or long distance. In those days the kids that ran long distance were children of parents who came to the US from Central Europe like Poland andCzecheslovakia. Their fathers ran Cross Country and the mile and two mile as kids in Europe.

John's parents were big time into sports enthusiast specially baseball. They lived close to Prospect Park. John and his Dad would toss around the baseball from time to time there. John would play baseball and football at an area called The Parade Grounds. There were many baseball diamonds on the Grounds and that switched to football fields in the fall. When it was cold in the winter the lake in Prospect Park would freeze over and John could play ice hockey there.

John's parents were very business savvy. His Mom owned her own business, a shop in Brooklyn that sold kitchen stuff like dishes and glassware. She was especially productive after the end of WWII. Lots of money to spend. His dad owned a few butcher stores. Everybody that met his Dad loved him. He had a great sense of humor.

Both John and Pete went to Public High Schools their first two years. Pete went to a public academy in Brooklyn his last two years and John went to Prep school in Pennsylvania his last two years. John was an excellent student but he felt that the Public School was too easy and therefore he would have a hard time getting into a good college. One of John's cousins, Jimmy, went to Prep School so John's parents asked Jimmy's parents about how to get into that school. They found that they could afford the tuition so they asked John if he wanted to go. John had mixed emotions about that as he did not want to leave all his friends in Brooklyn and his girlfriend to go far away to school. John had not given much thought as to what he would do after college. He did have a leaning towards the Medical profession especially as a Pathologist. He felt he did not have the required bedside manner to be a Family Doctor but did like the idea of research and the study of anatomy so he decided to go to the Prep School. The summer before going to Prep School he worked as a waiter at a kid's sleep camp away in Pennsylvania He received good tips from the parents at the end of camp because the kids really liked him.

CHAPTER THREE

John did very well at Prep School. The students came from all over the United States and some from overseas. Some of the friendships he acquired remained a part of his adult life. He managed to make the track team running the I/2 mile. He was a bit competitive but never won a race. He finished in the top five in grade point average. When it came time for the Senior Prom he invited his first true love in Brooklyn to the dance. Unfortunately she did not feel the same about him. He was proud to show her off to his classmates She was a stunner.

John decided to be a Pre-Med student at the University of Pennsylvania. He applied to five different Colleges and was accepted by all. In his first year one of the courses he took was Qualitative Analysis, a Chemistry course. From the get go he was completely lost so he decided that if he passed the course he would transfer to the Wharton School. Lucky for him if he could do that. He hired a tutor and passed the course. In his Sophomore year at Penn he joined the same fraternity that his cousin Jimmy was in. The fraternity had the highest grade point average of any of the 38 on campus.

Towards the end of his 2nd year at Penn, right before final exams, John decided to join the Air Force. He quit school and took all is stuff home to his parents place and said his goodbyes. His parents were not very happy about this but there was nothing they could do. He was sent to Lackland Airbase in San Antonio Texas. It was so crowded there that he and others would sleep on the runways. He trained on A10 planes before he got to fly jets. The fighter plane of choice in the Air Force was the F86 which was a joy to fly. The training was very difficult especially in the heat of the summer. At least half of the Cadets did not make it to the end. This was in the middle of the Korean War so after flight school he was shipped to South Korea where he flew more than 22 missions. Many of the pilots did not make it home alive as John thought that the Chinese pilots were superior to the American Pilots. The training at Lackland was very tough but he thought that he was well equipment to take on the Chinese. He never shot down an enemy plane nor did he have many close calls to be shot down. It seemed like the whole time he was in Country it rained which made flying a bit more difficult but he managed ok.

CHAPTER FOUR

After spending two years in the Air Force, John went back to Penn and to the Wharton School. He did very well, grade wise, with a 4.2 average which helped his Fraternity to be number one. In order to finish in two years, he went to summer school the summer before his Junior year and also before his Senior year. He became very interested in the Stock Market in his Senior Year and decided to try for a job with Merrill Lynch. In the meantime, he was made the Social Chairman for his fraternity. He booked the bands for the Saturday night parties and bought the beer for the parties. He also selected the favors the brothers would give their dates at special party occasions.

At the beginning of his Senior year, he met and dated the girl that would become his wife. JO was a wonderful girl and they were immediately attracted to each other. He was 23 and she was 19 They were married in the afternoon of graduation day and drove to Brooklyn there after. Some time before their marriage they drove to Brooklyn to rent an apartment. John had saved some money from his Air Force days so they would be ok.

He took the Subway on Monday to Merrill Lynch office on Pine Street He had made an appointment to take a series of tests and to be interviewed for the job of Account Executive. To his delight he was offered a job to go into training in New York. It would be a 6 month program. He wanted to work in Texas so they told him that he would go to the Dallas office upon completion of his training. John and Jo found out that she was pregnant at the time of his start of training. John and Jo decided to move to Dallas a month before training was over so they flew to Dallas on a long weekend to lease an apartment and to find a Doctor to deliver their baby. The manager of the Dallas office was very helpful in their dealing with the apartment and finding a Doctor, It all worked out well.

They sent their furniture to Dallas after training was over and set up housekeeping He learned a lot about prospecting in training and was anxious to begin his job as an Account Executive Shortly after arriving in Dallas they welcomed their daughter. His Mom flew to Dallas to help Jo with the baby which was welcomed support. They did not have a lot of money being paid only $265 per month plus commission. Jo took a job as apartment complex manager which cut their rent in half and was very helpful. Jo took care of the baby while John was at work,

CHAPTER FIVE

They could only afford one car so on his trips to see prospects and clients he sometimes had to use public transportation. Mostly he would be making cold calls on the telephone day and night and even on weekends. Out of 100 phone calls he was able to develop 10 prospects and of the 10 prospects he got 3 to4 accounts. He was happy with his progress but he put in very long hours. After one year he was making about $25000 which was above average. They were finally able to purchase their second car which gave John more flexibility. In addition John was entered into The President's club which gave him some perks such as a membership to a Country Club and a yearly comprehensive physical. Things were going well for John and Jo. They loved their life so much in Dallas that Jo's parents decided to move there. They were retired and it meant baby sitters for John and Jo so their social life would improve.

One day John's manager walked into his office with a young man. He introduced the man as Dayton Hudson who wanted to open an account. John was pleased that the manager gave him a new account. John spent the next several hours interviewing Mr. Hudson. Dayton was 6 foot 3 inches weighing 210 pounds and was 22 years old. He was a Professional Ice Hockey player playing for the Dallas Avengers, a farm team of the Toronto Maple Leafs. Dayton grew up in Windsor Ontario Canada He has played hockey as a little kid and played Junior Hockey before being drafted by the Maple Leafs. He was married and to his High School sweetheart, Maude who was 22 Since they had no children, Maude worked as a receptionist at Taylor Publishing. He had some discretionary money that he would like to invest in the market. John talked to Dayton about his risk tolerance. Dayton said that he was risk adverse and wanted to invest in stocks. When John began his career as a Account Executive he decided to be very conservative with his recommendations being more aggressive once he understood the risk tolerance of his clients. Dayton wanted to invest $10,000 right then with the possibility of more as time went on. John made several recommendations which Dayton accepted and so the account was opened. No question that the two guys were pleased with the relationship. Over time Dayton put more money into the account and John did a very good job for Dayton. Over time Dayton referred a few of his teammates to John which John appreciated. Most of the new accounts that John got were as referrals from existing clients.

The first stock John recommended to Dayton was Shakespeare, a fishing rod company. He purchased 500 shares at 7 ¼ and sold at 14 ½ so he doubled his money.

He had good luck on most of the investments John recommended.

CHAPTER SIX

Jo was pregnant with their second child. John was hoping for a boy this time that he could teach him about athletics. They did a sonogram in her 6th month and it was a boy. John was delighted big time. John's business continued to improve and his manager would give him some accounts from time to time. His client base continued to increase which, of course, led to more production. John was entering his 2nd year at Merrill and his income was about $55,000,

John relationship with Dayton Hudson had become a social relationship. The two couples would go out to dinner and to a movie from time to time. They really enjoyed each others company. Dayton and his wife Maude were frequent guest to John's home for dinner. Dayton would give John tickets to some of their games John really appreciated the tickets. Dayton was always picking John's mind about business in general. When John questioned Dayton about his interest, Dayton replied that he wanted to be able to get into some kind of business in his home town when he retired from Hockey. John was eager to provide a lot of what he learned at Wharton and his experience working at Merrill Lynch.

From time to time Dayton would invite John to be a part of the Avenger's practices. John was a very good skater and enjoyed the opportunity. Dayton's coach and his teammates were ok with John being there. Every once and a while during those practices Dayton would run John into the boards not to hurt him but just for fun. Now John weighed 175 and Dayton weighed 210. John did not think that it was funny.

CHAPTER SEVEN

At one of Dayton's visit to John's office, Dayton related that he had a broken bone in one of his feet. It was painful to play. The team trainer gave Dayton some pain killers but they did not work. John had migraine headaches and took a controlled substance, Percodan, for the headaches and they worked. So John gave Dayton 3 pills out of his stash to try. Dayton took them over the next few games and they worked but they were so strong that he could not remember much about the game. Since the pills worked John gave him 9 pills in an old prescription bottle.

After about a week or ten days went by Dayton called John to tell him that the team trainer found the pill bottle and reported that to the team coach. The coach reported that to the team general manager who in turn reported it to the league. Dayton was put on suspension until they heard from the league. The league called this morning and suspended Dayton for the rest of the season.

John was worried so he called his attorney, Paul Bass. He had met Paul at a social event sponsored by the Avengers and they had become friends. Paul said that John will probably hear from the authorities shortly and to call him when that happens. The law is pretty hard on any sort of distribution of a controlled substance. The next day two Sherriff Deputies arrived at John's office, handcuffed him and took him to jail. John was so embarrassed, he hung his head in shame as they took him away. At the Police station they finger printed him and took pictures and allowed him to make the one phone call. John's wife had no idea of what took place regarding the pills going to Dayton so when she heard from John that day that he had been arrested she was very upset. John asked her to call Paul to let him know that John had been arrested.

Paul came to the police station and found out that John was to be charged before a Judge the next morning. There would be a bail amount set by the Judge at that time. Paul gave John that information and said he would be back in the morning.

The nest morning John and Paul appeared before the Judge. The Judge set bail at $100,000 asked John how he pleaded and John replied not guilty. Paul called Jo to tell her what had taken place and that she had to bring $10,000 to a bail bondsman so that John could be bailed out. The trial was set in two months giving Paul time to come up with a defense.

CHAPTER EIGHT

When John was bailed out he called Dayton to let him know about the coming trial. Dayton felt badly and told John that he and Maude would be going back home to Canada to serve the suspension. John told Paul what Dayton had said and Paul asked John to bring Dayton to his office before he left town. They did meet but Paul found no help from Dayton to shore up the defense. He did tell Dayton that he needed to be prepared to come back to Dallas to appear as a witness at the trial.

Over the next few weeks Paul tried to come up with a good defense for John. He went through law books to try and find some precedence that would help but found none. Paul needed to have a serious conversation so they got together one afternoon. Paul said that the only defense he could come up with fell far short of what could help John. So the result was that John needed to plead guilty and hope that he would receive a very light sentence as John was a first time offender. Of course John was crushed.

The day of the trial came and John plead guilty. The Judge sentenced him to 1 to 3 years in prison. John could not believe that he was going to jail. Paul tried to assure him that with good behavior he might be out in less than one year. John hugged Jo and they took him away. She was in tears and didn't know what life would be without John.

Jo parents were in the courtroom at the time of the sentencing. They comforted Jo and said she needed to support John while he was in prison. She did not look forward to visiting him in jail. She had never been to a jail. What to tell the kids? She told them that their Dad would be going to a far away city and would not be back for a year. The children seemed to buy the story and would be reinforced with letters from their Dad.

CHAPTER NINE

John was taken immediately to the State prison in Huntsville. On the way there all John could think of was this must be a bad dream and he would awake soon. When he got to prison they gave him his clothing plus sheets and blanket plus a towel. He was disrobed of his street clothes and sent to the shower to bathe. After he was taken to a cell with only one bed in it plus a sink and a toilet. Soon a man in a suit came to see him and he turned out to be the Warden. The warden explained all the rules of the prison and that, except for meals, he would be confined for all but one hour a day where he could be outside in the courtyard. He also told him that, at least for the time being, he would be assigned to the library. All John could think of was this was all overwhelming. How could he spend the next year of his life under these conditions? Hopefully Paul would press for a new trial but that would be a stretch. He hoped that Jo would visit him from time to time and that she and the kids would be ok.

In about an hour or so the bell rang and the door to his cell opened up and everyone was in line to go to the mess hall for dinner. He looked around and saw all kinds of individuals who looked scary to him. He realized that there were rapists and murderers and all kinds of criminals here with him 24 seven. What a way to spend the next year. The food was awful but he knew he had to eat to keep his strength up which would be difficult. Could he make friends with some of the inmates or would be wary of everyone? He heard lots of bad stories of prison life and that worried him. It was all too hard to process. After dinner everyone went back to their cells to do whatever. He had nothing to read. There was no TV and no radio. So all he could do was think and then await lights out and try and sleep. He did not sleep well and then early in the morning the bell rang again and it was time for breakfast and for the lines to form again.

After breakfast he was told that he could spend the next hour shaving and showering but he had no soap or shaving stuff so he did not know what to do. He asked one of the guards about having no stuff to shave and shower and he was told that he could buy that stuff at the commissary. John had only a few dollars to spend so he bought a few things including a pen and writing paper and soap and a razor. He would write a note to Jo asking her to bring stuff to him as soon as possible.

It was time for him, after spending an hour in the courtyard, to go to the library to work. He was very cautious and did not talk to anyone. Was this the way it would always be? The library was fairly large and he was introduced to the head librarian who was just another prisoner like him. He asked the guy what he was supposed to do and he was told that he would wheel a cart with various books on it to the cells and ask if anyone wanted a book to read. So he loaded up the cart with books that the head guy gave him and went to the cell blocks to do his job. Looked like it would take both morning and afternoon to visit all the cells. Is this what he would do everyday? Pretty boring. So on his way he went. He was greeted by lots of shouting like "Whose the new guy? What happened to Johnny? Don't you have any better books? Not a great way to spend his first day at work.

Everyday was a repeat of the day before. He did help himself to a few books from the library which would give him something to do while in his cell at night after dinner. After a week went by Jo had not visited

 PHILIP STEPHENS

him so he was very disappointed but the next day he was told he had a visitor. He was taken to the visiting area which was divided by Plexiglas's with the visitor on one side and himself on the other. He was happy to see Jo there and told that she had brought a care package with her that would be given to him after being looked at for contraband. Jo tried to smile and let him know that the kids were fine and she was getting along ok. She told him she had put a few dollars into his Canteen account. The meeting lasted about 20 minutes and then she was gone. John was somewhat taken back about what he thought was a bit standoffish on Jo's part but he was glad to get the care package.

CHAPTER TEN

In the meantime Dayton and Maude were back to Windsor and stayed with friends till they could find an apartment. Their furniture was in storage in Dallas and would be shipped to Windsor when they found an apartment.

Dayton was still rocked by the decision of the League to suspend him for the rest of the season for about 4 months without pay would be a problem. Maude can easily find a job as she has good secretarial skills. For Dayton it would be difficult. Maybe he could find a job as an assistant coach in Hockey. He would get the word out to friends that he needed to get a job preferably in Hockey. If he got a paying job, he would devote some time to coaching Hockey for local teams.

He was upset that sometime in the next few months he would have to fly back to Dallas to testify at John's trial. He really felt sorry for the state of affairs for John. He did know that John had plead guilty and was sentenced to 1 to 3 years in prison. When he did find out he was really upset for John. How will he be able to handle prison life?

Even though Dayton did not have a job, he was still very much interested in going into business in Windsor. His long term goal was to own as many bars and pool halls as he could. He knew it would take big bucks to accomplish his goal. His plan was to buy one at a time as he had money to do that He intended to ask his hockey friends to be minority owners for a cash infusion. In addition he would do the same deal with friends and family. He secretly hoped that someday maybe he and John could be partners,

Dayton wished that John were here to help him to do the work necessary to accomplish his goals. He remembered John's advice in starting a business and that would be to have a comprehensive marketing plan including the potential income that each new business would generate.

Without John's support it would be a difficult task. He sat down and wrote a letter to John asking for him to send him an outline of what the marketing plan would look like. He called John's attorney in Dallas to get an address for John so he could send John that letter. In back of Dayton's mind was the thought that when John gets out of prison he could move to Windsor and be a partner with him.

CHAPTER ELEVEN

D ayton's first order of business was to find a job so he registered with several employment agencies. He was willing to accept any job that would produce decent income and give him time to raise some money to buy his first business. He had received the address from Mr. Bass to write to John.

John received the letter from Dayton and was very pleased that he could help him acquiring a business. He also relished the idea that it would give him something to really work on. John needed to get supplies from the Canteen including lots of paper. There was a typewriter in the library which he could use to put his plan in print to send to Dayton. John was always worried about what he would do after prison. Dayton's plan to build an empire in Windsor appealed to John. He could be a big help in that plan so maybe he might think about asking John if he wanted a partner. Would Jo be willing to move to Canada?

Over the next few weeks John spent a lot of time writing about that marketing plan plus some other comments. The more he wrote the more excited John got about moving to Canada after prison. The next time JO visits he would get her thoughts about a possible move to Canada and the opportunity to work with Dayton.

Over the next few months, Dayton got a number of job leads and went on several interviews. There were several jobs that appealed to him but he wanted to look for maybe better choices. One of his thoughts

PHILIP STEPHENS

was maybe to work as a bar tender at either a bar or at a pool hall to give him a better idea of how the system worked at these facilities. After continuing to look at job opportunities he was offered a job as a bar tender at the most popular pool hall in Windsor. The money was ok but he knew that getting good tips was where the money was. He accepted the job and began to work immediately.

CHAPTER TWELVE

John's brother, Pete, was doing very well down in Florida working for Merrill Lynch. He was just made a Manager for one of their offices in Miami-Dade County. Pete fancied himself as a stand up comedian in fact he did spend some weekends doing stand up at a Comedy Club in Miami. Pete was well liked by everyone at Merrill in Florida. Whenever they had a corporate meeting in Florida or regions around the country, Pete was always asked to be the Master of Ceremonies and always did a fine job.

When Pete found out about his brother, he was completely dismayed and he thought his brother was too smart to do what he did. It did not make a lot of sense to Pete. Pete wanted to do what he could to support John. He would write to him and, if possible, call him on the phone. Perhaps he might take a long weekend and visit John in the prison. Other than that he had no idea what else he could do. He thought he might call John's attorney and get the straight scoop on what was happening and how long he thought John would have to stay in prison. Pete was also concerned about what John would do after prison to earn a living. He would give some thought to that concern.

Pete did call Jo and get her perspective on the situation. He had not talked to her in a very long time. When he called, he found Jo to be somewhat standoffish and not very receptive. He worried about what their relationship looks like now and what it would be for them after prison. He just could not get a handle on what Jo was thinking and what her plans night be. Perhaps when he was in touch with John either by mail or phone, he would get a better idea of where that relationship stood. He was concerned also about his niece and nephew and how they were handling the situation.

CHAPTER THIRTEEN

Several months have gone by and Jo is less inclined to visit John in prison. She continues to seek the advice of her parents who seem to be considering Jo's getting a divorce because the future does not seem to be positive for John and Jo once he gets out of prison. Jo has not visited John for several months and John is unhappy not seeing his wife. He speculates that Jo's parents are having a negative affect on Jo.

John has made a few friends, if you can call them friends, over the past several months. He does not feel comfortable talking to any about his situation. Phone calls from his parents and brother are well received so at least his family is providing positive reinforcement in addition to the letters from them.

John has worked hard on replying to Dayton about business matters. He has sent a number of ideas to Dayton and the response from Dayton has been positive. The responses from Dayton speak to the possibility of John and Dayton be in some sort of partnership which delights John. He still is worried about how Jo would feel about moving to Canada.

In the meantime Dayton is working hard and accumulating some money from his job. He has also gotten some idea of what it would cost to start a business. He has had several conversations with his banker friend regarding getting a loan to buy a pool hall. He has also sent out feelers to his friends, relatives and Hockey buddies. These feelers were general in scope waiting to get a better idea of how much money he would have to raise.

John received a letter from Paul indicating that there is not enough information that could generate an appeal of his sentence. Paul also encouraged John to stay out of trouble and try to be positive about the future. Although the news from Paul was not encouraging he was pleased that Paul has kept in touch.

John has used the typewriter in the library not only to send stuff to Dayton but to send letters to his family including his kids. No one has asked to use the typewriter so John can use it whenever he wants to. Finally after quite a few months have gone by he is resigned to the schedule of events on each day with every day being a carbon copy of the day before. The days seem to move quickly which is positive for John. He has a monthly calendar where he can cross off each day before going to sleep at night.

When some of his fellow prisoners found out that he used to be a stock broker, they would bring questions to John about the markets. He has gotten permission from the Warden to hold a weekly meeting on the markets where inmates could attend. John enjoyed those sessions even though there was not a huge gathering. Sometimes the inmates would pay John for his advice.

CHAPTER FOURTEEN

Six mounts have flown by and John continues to hold up well. He has not been bullied by any of the inmates and he is thankful for that. Jo has decided, after much input from her parents, to seek a divorce and sell their home and move in with her parents for the time being. Her folks have a huge home with plenty of room for Jo and the kids. She would keep John's share of the sale of the home in escrow until he gets out of prison. In her letter to John she explained all the above but she did not know the sale price at that time. She also said that after he leaves prison he would have generous time with the children. They also had a portfolio of stocks which amounted to about $45000 which John asked her to sell from the joint account at Merrill and put half of it into her name and the other half into the escrow account.

There is nothing John could do to stop the divorce as all the "cards" were in Jo's hands. He expected this to happen so he wasn't too upset. He was still a young man so he would have plenty of opportunities for relationships after he got out of prison. He called his parents to tell them the news and that he was ok with the divorce. He also called Paul asking him to examine the divorce papers to make sure everything was in order in terms favorable as possible for John.

He no longer had to worry about whether or not Jo would be of to move to Canada. He called Dayton to let him know about the divorce.

He asked Dayton to call Paul to write a document regarding John and Dayton's partnership and he hoped it would be a 50-50 deal.

Dayton was surprised at the pending divorce. He thought that the marriage was strong enough to withstand the current events. He was overjoyed to learn that John would be coming to Canada and to be a huge part of the coming partnership. He would be ok with the 50-50 arrangement as John brought so much support into the business as shown by all the ideas John had been sending to him. So the next day Dayton called Paul asking him to set up a Partnership agreement for John and himself on a 50-50 basis. John would be responsible for the financial parts of the business and marketing while Dayton would run the business on a daily basis and hoped that John would be satisfied with the agreement.

CHAPTER FIFTEEN

John received a copy of the Partnership agreement from Paul and felt it was ok with him. There is a copy machine in the library so he used it to copy the agreement and send it to Dayton. John was really excited about what would take place after he got out of prison. The days would pass quickly and that his good behavior will get him out after a year. He could only hope that would be the case.

In the meantime Dayton remains very active. He is enjoying his job at the Pool Hall learning a bunch about how things operate. He also was trying to find out what the going prices were to buy bars and pool halls. He didn't want to be too obvious so he was being careful not to set off any alarms. Dayton also continued to meet with his banker friend trying to get an idea how much money he could borrow. There needed to be a cash infusion from John and Dayton when they make a loan application. He was also interested to know what the rate of interest would be needed to make the loan, Another reason why he needed that interest information was to let investors know what they would earn interest wise. The deal would have John and Dayton as the General Partners and every one else be Limited Partners.

John had asked Paul to set up a legal document for the partnership outlining who the General Partners would be and what the Limited Partners would look like including the amount of annual interest to be paid to the Limited Partners which will not be known until the bank

PHILIP STEPHENS

tells Dayton what John and Dayton would pay. Regarding the down payment the money that was being held in escrow for the sale of John's house would be part of the down payment. John has asked Jo to tell him how much was in that account. Since there was a small mortgage on the home, the proceeds from the sale would be impacted by the mortgage. John's hope is that it would be substantial considering the quality of the home and the neighborhood and the small mortgage. He could only hope awaiting the info from Jo.

Dayton was pleased that John was spending a good deal of time in preparation for their first purchase in Windsor. He called Paul to say that he was ok with the document regarding the partnership.

CHAPTER SIXTEEN

John has received the divorce papers from Jo which he signed and sent back to her. He heard from Jo the amount of money in the escrow account amounted to $87,000 which was great as it would be needed, in part, for the down payment for their first purchase. John passed that information along to Dayton. He also asked Dayton to provide him as much information he had on what they would need to buy their first Pool Hall. Time was marching on and the end of the first year was almost upon him. He was somewhat apprehensive not knowing what Paul would be doing to get him out of there at the end of the year,

John asked Dayton to scout out some apartments John could lease when he arrived in Windsor. He would need a car also, probably a used one. John could deal with that when he gets there. Would they be working out of Dayton's house? So many questions but they had time on their side to firm up the necessary initial plans.

Paul was constantly in touch with John or Dayton about John's possible release after positive conversations with the Dallas District Attorney and the Warden at the prison. Paul decided not to send a bill to Dayton for his services. That could wait until the guys are settled in Windsor. Paul had a conversation with the Parole Board about John moving to Canada when he was paroled. The board felt they could accommodate John. He was also in touch with John's parents and his brother telling them he believes John will only have to serve one year.

CHAPTER SEVENTEEN

John continues to do his job at the library knowing that the parole board is set to meet in a few days. Everyone involved seems to feel that John will be paroled. John is preparing himself for that meeting It will be held at the prison tomorrow. John could hardly get any sleep that night before the meeting but he is ready and able to put up a good face at that meeting.

The day of the meeting is here. John is ushered into the conference room next to the Warden's office. He is seated before three judges with the Warden near the front. They ask John if he believes he is ready to be in the community again and that he has learned the error of his ways. John response is a very positive yes to all those kinds of questions. The judges turn to the Warden and ask him if he believes John is rehabilitated and that he should be paroled. The Warden says that John has been a model prisoner and in his opinion he should be paroled. Usually the three judges take some time to make a decision but in this case the immediately vote three to none to grant John immediate parole.

John, of course, is delighted with the ruling and asks the Warden what are the next step The warden replies that he needs to inform the Dallas District Attorney and make sure that there is no reason not to release John immediately. That should take few hours and if everything stays as it is John would be released tomorrow. John was excused from the meeting and taken back to his cell. John asks if he could call his attorney to come and get him tomorrow and he is granted that call. Paul is overjoyed at the news and said he would be there.

When the morning comes the Warden tell John that the DA in Dallas is ok with the pardon. He also said that the Parole board will allow John to move to Canada and the meetings with his parole officer could be done by either phone or by Skype. John was getting his stuff together pending his release. He had a small savings account which was given to him plus whatever he had on him when he was entering prison. So all was in order and at 10AM John was released to his attorney Paul Bass. It was a joyful reunion.

John had asked Paul to get him a motel room which he could use while he was still in Dallas and secondly how to get the money that was in escrow from the sale of his house. Paul said that he had already arranged for a hotel room for John and that the escrow account only needed John's signature.

Paul drove John to the bank where the escrow money was being held. John signed the document and deposited the money into an account that had checking. They signed him up and gave him temporary checks he could use. John had his Texas drivers license as proof of who he was. He needed to go to the store and buy clothing and shoes and underwear plus go to the drug store to buy shaving stuff. He also needed to buy suitcases to store his stuff moving to Canada, They stopped for something to eat before going to the several stores. He spent about $2000 for his purchases and was pleased.

John needed to lease a car that he could take to Canada. Paul knowing that had made the necessary arrangements for John to get the car. They drove to the rental place where John got the car and placed all his purchases in the car. John needed to meet with Paul in regard to any documents he needed to take to Canada so he made an appointment to meet the next morning at Paul's office. They said their goodbyes and took off. He forgot that he needed to get a cell phone so he stopped at a Verizon store and bought a new cell phone.

CHAPTER EIGHTEEN

When John got to the hotel he needed help to move all his stuff to his room. The desk provided someone to help him. Upon his arrival he unpacked everything and again was pleased with his purchases as he put them in his closet. The first thing he did was to call Dayton in Canada. Dayton was pleased John was free and asked when he would come to Canada. John said he needed a few days to finish some things and would call back when he was on his way. Would Dayton arrange for a place for him to stay temporarily in Canada and Dayton said ok. He told Dayton that he would be meeting with Paul the next day to get any documents he had regarding the partnership.

Paul had given Jo's phone number to John so he called her. John told her that he was a free man. She was happy for him. John wanted to make an appointment to come and see the kids. He wanted to do that tomorrow.

.She said the kids would be home from school at 3 so he could come then. John took $1000 cash from the bank as he would not get a credit card until he gets to Canada.

He had dinner in the hotel and charged it to his room. After dinner he went back to his room and made a list of what he had to do. Most of the things on the list he had already done so he felt good about where he was. He felt a bit apprehensive about seeing his kids after a year and what he should tell them.

The next morning he ate breakfast in the dining room and then made his way to Paul's office. The first matter of business was what was Paul's fee at this point. He wrote a check for half the amount and told Paul to invoice Dayton for the other half.

There were several documents that Paul gave to John. The first was a final draft on the partnership agreement between John and Dayton. The second was the Limited Partner document which would be given to the Limited Partners after an interest rate was decided on. That appeared to be what was needed so John thanked Paul for all he had done for him and Dayton and said he would be in touch. They shook hands and John left the office. He had several hours before he needed to go Jo's home so he went back to the hotel and made several phone calls.

The first was to his parents to tell them about his release and his pending move to Canada. He told them he was going into business with Dayton and they could tell by his voice how excited he was about the move, They wished him well and would talk to him soon. The other call was to Pete in Florida. Pete was happy to hear the news about John's release. John told him about the new business venture that John would be a part of. He went on further to tell him that it was a Partnership deal with himself and Dayton as General Partners and hopefully lots of Limited Partners who would be paid quarterly interests payments. He hoped that Pete would be a Limited Partner. Pete wished John lots of luck and hoped he would hear from him soon.

It was time to go to see the kids so he left the hotel and proceeded to that appointment. He was still conflicted about what to tell the kids. Jo greeted John at the door and welcomed him into her home. The kids seemed to be generally glad to see their Dad which put John at ease. He hugged both kids and asked if he could be with them alone. Jo agreed. John told the kids that he missed them but he was going away again. He promised to keep in touch with them and would see them soon again.

They seemed confused so John told them that his business was taking him to another city far away. He hugged the kids again, said his goodbyes to them and to Jo. He promised he would be in touch with Jo giving her his new address and phone number.

 PHILIP STEPHENS

CHAPTER NINETEEN

After leaving Jo's it was about 4PM too early for dinner so he decided to cruise around the city for the next few hours, He was really sad to be leaving Dallas and Texas.

He got to see some of his favorite sights in Dallas like Dallas Cowboy Stadium, Reunion Arena, Park Cities and many others He decided to have dinner at his favorite restaurant Bob's Steak and Chop House. When he arrived there he was greeted by the head waiter who said " Its been a while. Where have you been?" John responded by saying "I've been out of town for over a year." John ordered his favorite steak and onion rings and a bottle of his favorite wine. He only drank half the bottle and thoroughly enjoyed his meal especially the signature item of the house; a glazed carrot. John said goodbye saying he would see them in about a year. He drove back to his hotel happy with the day he had knowing that he would be leaving tomorrow. He did, however, stop at the bar and ordered his favorite after dinner drink a Grand Marnier which would provide him a good nights sleep.

He did,in fact, have a great nights sleep awaking at 8AM. He showered and got dressed and went down to the restaurant to eat breakfast. He ate a big breakfast as he would not stop for lunch on his way to Canada. After breakfast he went back to his room and called Dayton. Dayton answered and John told him he would be leaving shortly and would be in Windsor the day after tomorrow. He will call when he is in Windsor to get directions. He would see him soon.

He packed all his clothing and stuff into three suitcases and a garment bag and called the desk for help with his luggage. The porter came and took his luggage to the main floor. In the meantime John paid his bill in cash and had them bring his car to the front and put his luggage in the back of the SUV. John had gotten a map from Paul to direct him to Windsor so he was all set to leave Dallas.

He dove over to Highway 75 which would take him to Oklahoma, Kansas and Missouri. He would take his time as there was no rush and he did not want to get a ticket for speeding. It was now 8:30 in the morning and he hoped to get to St Louis by nightfall and spend the night there. The weather was perfect not a cloud in the sky. It was early June so it would not be too hot.

CHAPTER TWENTY

He had dressed casually as he would be in the car all day. He thought he would stop for gas when he gets into Oklahoma and get a few bottles of water at the same time. The was not much traffic after he left the outskirts of Dallas so he was driving comfortably. He had turned on a music station so he kept calm listening to the music. The road was very good being an interstate highway without very much to look at. No hills just pretty flat with lots of gas stations, apartment complexes and drive in restaurants. Everything was perfect.

After driving for a couple of hours he entered Oklahoma and the scenery was pretty much the same as in Texas. Still not much traffic except for a bunch of 18 wheelers.

He stopped at a Exxon station and purchased a few bottles of water. He wished he had a credit card instead of paying cash for everything. He went from 75 to 44 on the way towards Joplin Missouri It was now 1:30 in the afternoon so he stopped at a McDonalds for a hamburger and a soft drink and to use the men's room. In Joplin he was still on Route 44 on his way to Springfield and then to St Louis. It would still be light when he arrives in St Louis.

The road was still very good and the car was handling well. The scenery had changed to a more hilly environment and the traffic picked up after leaving Springfield. He was getting a bit tired since he had been on the road for about 7 hours. It was not too much further to his destination. It was about 6PM when he got out of his car and was on the outskirts of St. Louis deciding to stay at a Hamptons Inn for the evening. He checked into the motel and got a cart to take his luggage to the room because he did not want to leave it in the car. He asked about places to eat and was given a few choices. He chose Carrabas, an Italian restaurant that he had eaten at in Dallas years ago. It was 7PM when he entered the restaurant and it was pretty crowded. He ordered a beer and the some kind of pasta but no dessert. He did, however remember their Caesar Salad so he ordered that also. The food was good and he was finished by 8:15 looking forward to a good nights sleep and the anticipation of being in Windsor tomorrow. He though he would call Dayton before going to sleep to tell him where he was and to get directions once he gets to Windsor. Then, off to sleep.

The next morning he got direction to Windsor at the desk while he was paying the bill and it seemed simple enough going northeast from St Louis through Ft Wayne Indiana and near Detroit.

CHAPTER TWENTY ONE

Hampton Inn has a complimentary breakfast which John would take advantage of. pancakes, scrambled eggs and sausage was available. John ate a bunch knowing that he probably will not stop for lunch. The directions to Dayton' apartment were very specific and John should not have any trouble finding it. He had a good nights sleep and was anxious to get going. He had his luggage loaded on to the dolly and the porter took it all to the lobby. The luggage was loaded in John's car and he was more than ready to get going. The weather continues to be great with no rain in sight.

It was 8:30 and the traffic was very heavy getting out of St, Louis. Ft. Wayne was only several hours ahead and from there to Windsor would only be several hours also. He was really looking forward to see Dayton and Maude as it has been well over a year. He stopped just northeast of St. Louis for gas and a few bottles of water. The roads, as usual, were very good and his car continues to be perform well. Ft. Wayne showed up in a hurry and he was only a short drive to Windsor. He knew that he would be stopped at the border of Canada and they would no doubt ask what he was doing there. When the time came to cross the border they did ask him why he was going to Canada. His reply was that it was a business trip. He showed his passport which he remembered to carry with him. He was given safe passage.

It took about 1 hour to locate Dayton's apartment and he pulled up in front of the apartment complex. Really looked like an upscale facility. He got out of the car and made his way to Dayton's apartment and hit the doorbell. It was a big time greeting. Lots of hugging and pats on the back. Maude was there also to give hugs also. John was really pumped up to finally reach his destination.

Maude said to John that he was probably hungry and thirsty so she brought in a tray of sandwiches and iced tea.

They asked about his trip and John said it was a piece of cake and that was glad to finally be in Canada. They continued to visit and to eat the food. Dayton told John that they would deal with business affairs tomorrow and just relax today. He also told John that they would take his luggage tomorrow to the apartment that Dayton had leased for him. John did not want to leave his luggage in the car so Dayton helped him to bring it all to his apartment.

It was getting close to dinner time. Dayton suggested that they go out to dinner at a nearby restaurant which John agreed to. They visited a bit more and then made their way to the restaurant. A quaint little Italian restaurant was where they would eat. They all enjoyed their meal which included beer for everyone. Their apartment had a second bedroom which John was to use. They hit the hay not to long after returning from dinner. John was keyed up so it took a while for him to fall asleep.

CHAPTER TWENTY TWO

The next morning Maude fixed breakfast and they all ate well. Dayton said that both he and Maude had taken off the day to be with John. John asked about his new apartment and Dayton said they would go there after breakfast. They loaded up John's car and headed to the apartment. On the way Dayton gave him some facts about the apartment including the monthly rent which was acceptable to John. Dayton also said that he had leased a furnished apartment to make it simple for John to move in. They brought all the luggage to the apartment which was on the ground floor. John was very happy with the way the apartment looked and said he would live there for a while to see if he liked it. If not, he could move.

He looked in the fridge and the pantry and to his surprise they were fully stocked. He was overwhelmed and thanked John and Maude for the trouble it took to accomplish that. John had a short list of things he needed to do right then. Most importantly was to set up a bank account so Dayton took John to his bank and introduced him to his banker. John needed a credit card and to set up an account with checking privileges The bank needed to get his money from Dallas to deposit here. He signed a bunch of papers and the banker excused himself for a bit. When he came back he had a few temporary checks and a Visa credit card for John. The banker told him that the funds from Dallas would be there tomorrow. John was amazed how everything was taken care of so quickly.

John also needed to get a new cell phone company with a new phone number so they went to the nearest cell phone provider and set John up with that new phone and number. Dayton suggested that John wait until later in the day to unpack as they need to spend some time on business matters. So they got into John's car and drove back to Dayton's apartment.

John gave Dayton a copy of the agreed upon Partnership Document and asked if he was still ok with the agreement and, if so, it needed to be signed in the presence of a notary. The second document was the Limited Partnership agreement which would be given to those who have an interest in investing their money. Did Dayton know at what interest rate his bank was going to charge us for the loan to purchase our first property? Dayton replied that the interest rate would be 4% and that is what we will pay the Limited Partners. He went on further to say that the Partnership document is fine with him and we can take it to the bank this afternoon to sign it and have it notarized, As far as the Limited Partnership document is concerned, after we plug in the interest rate, we need have copies printed to have at the ready.

CHAPTER TWENTY THREE

t was about noon and time to eat lunch so they decided to take a break and Maude provided them with sandwiches and bottled water. The elephant in the room was how much Dayton could put into the business as they needed some money in the partnership bank account that needed to be set up so after lunch John posed that question to Dayton. Dayton responded by saying that he had surveyed the pool hall and bar environment and that it would cost about $100,000 to purchase either of them. They would have to put up about$40,000 to get a loan for $60,000 from the bank. So we need 40K plus some money to support out current needs so he was willing to put up $30000 at this time. John said that number was ok with him.

They needed to open an account with John's bank to put the $60000 in with check writing privileges. Dayton said that he had been in touch with potential investors and got good responses. He would take the Limited Partnership agreement to the printer and have 100 copies made to start with. John had made a list of potential clients from his old client list and Dayton had made a list of potential clients from the Hockey Community and friends and relatives.

John said the immediate need was to find a job for himself. He knew he could not be a bar tender like Dayton but did Dayton have any ideas. Dayton said he had a friend who owned an employment agency and he would call him and make an appointment for John for tomorrow morning. He would give John directions on how to get there. Dayton said they needed to go to the bank and have the Partnership document notarized. They also needed to go to the printer to get copies of the Limited Partnership agreement printed. So, off they went. They went to the bank first and signed the agreement and had it notarized. Then off to the printer where they asked to have 100 copies made of the Limited Partnership agreement. Dayton needed to go to work so John drove him home and returned to his apartment to unpack. They decided to meet for dinner at Dayton's apartment.

John went back to his apartment and started to unpack. He had not yet scoped out the apartment to get an idea of where everything was. There was plenty of room in the closet for John's clothing and the dresser gave him additional space. He checked the pantry and the fridge and made a list of groceries he needed to buy. When he was finished, he looked for the office of the manager of the complex to ask him several questions. Having found him, he wanted to know where the nearest grocery was and where the laundry was on the property. He got those questions answered and decided to hit the grocery store to purchase what was on the list.

CHAPTER TWENTY FOUR

One of the things he needed to ask Dayton about was did he have a computer. John would need one of his own to be in touch with potential clients and for general business. He could use his cell phone but a computer would be much more useful. John would have his money tomorrow so he needed to go to the bank along with Dayton to deposit the $60,000. John would go to a store and buy a computer and sign up with a provider using his old screen name and a new password plus purchase some software that was not a part of the provider's package. He needed things like Google and software to protect the computer from bad stuff. John was looking forward to the meeting with the employment agency to find a job. He had no idea what kind of work might be offered to him.

Evening came and John went to Dayton's home for dinner. they had a few beers and then sat down to a great meatloaf dinner with French fries and a salad. The meal was very much appreciated not having had a home cooked meal in forever. After dinner he approached Dayton about the computer and Dayton was ok with charging it to the business. He gave John the name of his provider and told him where the best place was to purchase a computer which made John happy. They made a date to meet at the bank at 3PM tomorrow to deposit the funds for the business. They decided that they needed to devote time each day to talking about progress in the business. That time would depend on available hours after or before work for two of them. Dayton shared with John that he had scoped out two possible pool halls for purchase. Maybe, as time permits, they could visit both of them the day after tomorrow They would touch base with each other tomorrow evening.

John was going to call Paul asking him to get email or snail mail addresses for the list of potential clients he would email to him after he gets a computer. Paul said his assistant could do that and he would send a bill for that service.

Seemed like there was so much to do but not to act to hastily for fear of making a mistake of sorts. Time was not a problem but doing things properly was important. First of all was to decide on what property to make a bid on and that would happen in the next few days.

CHAPTER TWENTY FIVE

John put on his best suit and tie and was prepared for his meeting with the employment agency. He arrived on time for the meeting and was greeted by a receptionist who inquired of his name. "John Drake here for a 10AM appointment". John was ushered into another office where a man was sitting behind a desk. The man introduced himself as Ron Walker friend of Dayton's.

Ron asked John to tell him about himself, age, where from, last occupation and what was he doing in Windsor. John gave him the answers to all Ron's questions. Ron wanted to know if there was any type of job that he wanted which John's said no. "Did you do anything else in your life other being a financial advisor? John said he was a waiter a long time ago. Ron looked through his list of job openings to try and find something that would fit with John. He did find several jobs as a waiter, several jobs as a telemarketer and, believe it or not, a job as an assistant at a local brokerage company. Ron told John about the job at a brokerage company and wanted to know if he could type since that was a requirement for the job. John said he took typing in high school and was a average typist. The job paid $1500 per month and would he be interested. Of course said John. Ron called the company and made an appointment for John to be interviewed in one hour. He got the name of the company and the directions how to get there. John didn't recognize the name. It was Royal Bank of Canada.

John went to the address and introduced himself to the receptionist as John Drake. The manager of the office came out to greet him and took John into his office. He asked John about his work history and John said he had been a financial advisor for a brief period of time in Dallas, Texas. He was in Windsor to be in a Partnership with Dayton Hudson which he did not have to spend much time with Dayton and his days were free and he needed a job. The manager asked him if he could type and he said he could but was average.

The manager said the job paid $1500 per month and the hours were 8AM to 5PM and would that suit him John said it was good. So they shook hands and asked him to fill out an brief application with his name address phone number and next of kin. He knew that John was not a Canadian so no money would be taken out of his paycheck except for government withholding. John did that in five minutes. They shook hands and he told John to be here tomorrow at 7:30 so he could introduce him to the people he would be working for. John said goodbye and that he would be here the next morning. What a break for John.

He left the office and headed for the store that sold computers. He selected a desktop which came with a monitor, keyboard and a mouse. He also bought a printer.

He needed to meet Dayton at 3PM when he could tell Dayton about the job. He also wanted to know who his internet provider was so he could sign up when he got home after the meeting.

CHAPTER TWENTY SIX

John called the bank to make sure the money was transferred to his new bank and he got confirmation. It was Thursday and he was looking forward to the weekend where he could do some work on the Partnership. He was hoping that Dayton would set up several meetings regarding the possible purchases of a bar and/or a pool hall. It was time to meet Dayton at their bank to make that deposit. He paid for the computer out of his own funds so he would have to get the money back.

Dayton was on time and they both wrote checks to be deposited in their business account. John's check was for $30000 minus the money he had spent on the computer et al. Dayton was ok with the purchase of the computer. He told John that he used AT& T as his provider and Norton for his safety net.

Dayton needed to be on his way to work so he excused himself and told John that they should get together on Friday morning at10AM at his apartment. John said that he would be working tomorrow and could meet at 6PM. John drove back to his apartment to work on his computer. He spent the next hour or so putting all the computer components together so he could use it right then. He first called AT&T to set up his TV service and to also set up the internet for his computer. He answered a lot of questions mainly about his credit card information. AT&T said they could be out there today at 5PM and that was good for John.

John got on the phone and called Paul hoping that he would still be in his office. Paul did pick up the phone. He told Paul about his new job and sounded very excited. He also told Paul that the Partnership was moving ahead and that they had accomplished a lot setting it up and in the planning stage. Had Paul gotten the info on the client names he asked him to ? Paul responded that they had some but not all and they were working on the rest. He was glad that things were moving along for John and Dayton. Please keep me up to date on what you have done. John said that he had just purchased a computer set up plus he had a new credit card and a new banker. They had just put $30000 each into the Partnership account mostly to pay for their first pool hall purchase. They have printed up 100 flyers about the Limited Partnership to send to prospective clients. Paul wished him good luck and hung up.

At 5PM on the nose the AT&T guy rang the doorbell. It took him about an hour to set everything up so John could begin to use the system. John thanked the service guy and led him to the door. John had the email addresses of his parents and his brother so he decided to drop them a line so they would know that everything was in order and that he had just been hired by Royal Bank of Canada to be a. broker assistant It did not take long to get a reply to his two emails and was happy to hear from his family. He also had Jo's email and sent her a note with his address and his new phone number in case she needed to be in touch.

CHAPTER TWENTY SEVEN

John had a Stouffer's frozen meal for dinner and then turned on the TV to look for a sporting event to watch. Fortunately the Stanley Cup Playoffs were on TV and the Toronto Maple Leafs were playing a game that evening so he watched the whole game which ended at about 10:30PM. Leafs won 3 to 1. He was tired so he went to sleep and set the alarm for 6:30 so he would have ample time to prepare for his first day of work. He showered and had a modest breakfast and was anxious to get going. He figured it would take about half an hour to get there so he left at 7:15 arriving a bit early.

When he arrived at his new office, his manager Jonathon, introduced him to the Account Executives he would be working for. They were two women, Sarah McGregor and Judy Campos. The women were both on the young side being in their 30's. Both were attractive which gave John a bit of a good feeling. The three of them had a brief meeting in the conference room where John told them about his experience in the brokerage business. They were both pleased with that information. They went on to tell him what they would expect from him. Firstly he needed to answer their phones if they were busy on other lines and to try and be helpful to the callers. From time to time they would need for him to type a letter or two. They knew that it would take a bit of time for John to learn about how things worked here but they would be patient with that process. They showed John where his desk was and went back to their individual offices.

John spent the day learning a bunch of stuff and answered many phone calls. Although things ran very differently than he was used to in Dallas, he could get the hang of it fairly quickly. He asked the ladies to give him a list of their biggest accounts which would help him do what was necessary. John wanted to know about lunch breaks and they said 45 minutes. Most of the employees brought their lunch from home and there was a soft drink machine in the break room. He just needed to tell them when he would be going to lunch. Since he did not bring his lunch, he asked where in the neighborhood he could get a sandwich so they directed him to that location.

The first day of work went very quickly and he was pleased with the progress he was making in learning what was necessary to get the job done in good order, At 5PM he asked if they needed any thing else and, if not, he would see them on Monday. He wished them a good weekend.

 PHILIP STEPHENS

CHAPTER TWENTY EIGHT

They needed to hire an attorney to be sure they were on good legal terms with setting up a Partnership with both General and Limited Partnerships. Dayton's brother in Law was an Attorney so they made an appointment to see him on Saturday afternoon at his office. They would bring along the document that Paul had put together. They would meet on Saturday at 10AM just to go over the two options they had to purchase a business.

The law in Ontario Canada says that a General Partnership can be created with the following stipulations:

1.   Registered trade name
2.   Registered Tax ID
3.   Bank account

Limited Partners can be part of the business and can only contribute money but have no say in the management of the business They need to confirm this with the attorney at their meeting to tell us if we were correct as to the legality of the Partnership. The attorney said that we were right on what was needed and he would do that for them and needed some information. They would use PHB Partnership as the trade name(Pool-Hall-Bars). I will send you a bill for my services after I get things done said the attorney. The meeting was adjourned.

Dayton and John continued to talk. Dayton wanted to take John to the two possible options this morning and then spend sometime deciding which one we liked. Off they went in Dayton's car to the first option. From the exterior it looked pretty good and the neighborhood was acceptable. They went inside the building to find a large space with at least 6 pool tables and fully stocked bar. It was early in the day so it was not crowded. John remarked that it looked ok to him but was anxious to see the 2nd option. The second option is where Dayton worked. It was very impressive from the outside and upon entering the building, they saw at least 8 pool tables and a bar area with good seating. The first option had a bar area also. They both said that they had seen enough so John said did Dayton have an idea of what it would take to purchase either option. Dayton replied that had a good idea of the cost of both options.

They got back to Dayton's apartment to discuss the choices. The first one would be around $85000 to $90000 and the second option would be around $110000. John's liked the 2nd option because of the layout and neighborhood. If we could buy the 2nd option for about $100000 that would be my choice. Dayton agreed, and since he worked there and knew the owner, he would contact him and set up a meeting to discuss the purchase. He thought he would offer $95,000 and see where it takes them. Dayton got on the phone and called the owner at the pool hall to set up the meeting. The appointment was to be at 3:30 in the afternoon.

CHAPTER TWENTY NINE

Since they were to meet at 3:30 Lunch was in order so Dayton drove to a place that had sandwiches John said it looked a lot like one in Dallas called Jimmy Johns. John ordered an Italian sub and a soft drink. Dayton ordered the same and they split the bill after really enjoying their lunch.

They arrived at the pool hall for their meeting with Jake Plummer, the owner, Dayton introduced John to him as his partner, We have an interest in buying your pool hall. Would you consider selling it if the price was right. Jake replied that he has owned this business for over 30 years and since he just turned 80 and was ready for retirement.

Dayton thanked Jake and said they would offer $95000 for the property. Jake countered at $105,000 and Dayton countered at $100,000. Jake said DEAL and they shook hands. John asked Jake under what name is the ownership called? Also what is the address and the name of the business?

Dayton said they would draw up the papers for the purchase and then consummate the purchase Please give him a few days to do that. They shook hands again and John and Dayton left the pool hall.

They went to Jason's home and were ecstatic about the purchase. Dayton said he would call his banker on Monday morning to set up the deal. There needs to be a closing with a Title company and a document regarding the nature of the sale. There was also a question of tax owned by Jake. The Title company would get that info. He hoped that his Banker would help them with all that.

John said that when Dayton sees the Banker he needs to get a credit card for both us under the name of the Partnership. They decided to go out to dinner to celebrate so Dayton picked a fancy French restaurant to go to. They would split the bill which was ok with John since they didn't have a company credit card.

They had a great time at dinner with lots of wine and good food. Both of the guys raised their glasses in a toast to their first purchase. Dayton said that tomorrow would be Sunday, a day of rest He would communicate with John Monday after meeting with the Banker. Dayton dropped John off at his apartment and said he would talk to him Monday.

CHAPTER THIRTY

John woke up at 8Am on Sunday. He called the desk and asked if they knew where the closest Episcopalian Church was. They answered about a mile. He got directions. He took a quick shower and headed for the Church. He arrived there at 8:50 and the service would start at 9AM. After the service was over he talked to the Rector and introduced himself to him. He gave the Rector a brief explanation as to why he was in Windsor and where he came from. He asked if he could be put on a mailing list of the activities at the Church. He gave the Rector the info he needed to accomplish that.

He had asked Dayton to recommend a good place to eat brunch on Sunday and Dayton gave him that information.

He headed that way and got there in 15 minutes. It was a huge place with lots of tables plus counter service. He chose to sit at one of the tables. When the waiter came John ordered a large orange juice plus pancakes, scrambled eggs and link sausage. He also wanted water. He took his time eating and enjoyed everything.

After brunch, he decided to drive around Windsor to get a better idea of the city. On his travels he saw a number of movie theatres, lots of restaurants, a large building that advertised a Hockey game for that afternoon. He thought it must be a junior league team but it could be one connected to the Maple Leafs. He drove past several large parks where people were picnicking and what appeared to be a large soccer stadium.

He got out of his car where there was an inviting park with benches. He noticed across the street a news stand so he bought the Sunday paper and took a seat in the park. It was a warm day in late June. The paper was not very large in volume but it was interesting to read it thoroughly and learned a lot about the city.

There was a large movie complex on the way home so he stopped to see a movie. There were four or five movies to watch so he chose the one that was about World War II.

He enjoyed the picture and it was over by 5PM. It was time to think about eating and he had noticed what looked like a diner near his apartment so he went in there to get a light dinner. After eating he drove back to his apartment and looked at the TV schedule he kept from the Sunday paper. There was a Maple Leaf game at seven PM and he would watch that,

It turned out to be a very fulfilling day getting to know more about his adopted city. From his drive he figured that the city was not very big but did not get to see many neighborhoods with single family homes. He would save that for another day. The game was over by ten so he decided to hit the sack and set his alarm to ring at 6:30AM.

CHAPTER THIRTY ONE

The first thing he did after getting up at 6:30 was to shower and shave. He had one of those coffee makers that you can set the time to brew so it was set for 7AM. He had cereal and fruit plus the coffee for breakfast. He made himself two tuna fish sandwiches and an apple to take to work for lunch. It was 7:45 when he left to go to work. He arrived at 8AM. He put his sandwiches in the fridge in the break room and went to his desk. There was a computer at his desk that he could use to get quotes on the New York and American Stock exchanges plus the Toronto stock exchange.

Both Sarah and Judy were at their desks already on their telephones. He knew that Dayton would be calling him late in the morning. He was anxious to hear from him. He spent most of the morning taking phone calls, putting them on hold for one of the ladies and giving quotes to callers. Sarah was opening a new account so she showed him how to fill one out so he could help her in the future filling out one.

At 11AM Dayton called and gave John a rundown of his visit with the Banker. He has two credit cards in the companies name and he will give one to John when he sees him. The Banker put together a Sellers agreement with a place to put in the Buyers agreement which includes Seller name and address and the price of sale and the buyers name and the name of the property. He also put him in touch with a

Title Company and he called them; Canadian Title Company. He gave them all the information about the sale and the possibility of tax liability. They said they would call both the buyer and seller to give them the closing date. It will in about a week. John was glad to get the news and he thanked Dayton for the work he did. The Banker will cut a check to us for $60000 the day before closing. Dayton wanted to get together this evening to be sure we have covered all the bases so could John be at Dayton's home at 6PM and John said he would be there.

The rest of the day went well for John continuing to learn about all the forms that are used and how the ladies would be using him. The ladies were being very patient with him which John appreciated. John left the office at 5:15 and headed to Dayton's apartment.

CHAPTER THIRTY TWO

ohn arrived at Dayton's at 5:45. Dayton gave him the company credit card. The PHB Company. It felt good to see that name on the card. John suggested that on Saturday they take another look at their purchased property to see what they needed to purchase in addition to what was in the office. They hoped that the owner would be there to introduce them to the employees. They also needed to get the salary information of the employees and any special arrangements he might have with any of the employees. They also needed the type of work each of the employees were responsible for.

John asked did Dayton notice if there was a computer in the office? If there was one could it be part of the sale of the business? If not they would have to buy one. John asked Dayton if he would go over the arrangements he made with the banker again. Dayton repeated it and it was very clear to John hearing it for the 2nd time. John said that he would work on the mailer that they would send to prospective Limited Partners. He would do that over the weekend. Does Dayton have at the ready a list of names and addresses of the people he wants to send the Pro Forma to? Dayton said he would do that over the weekend. John was thinking to himself that he had not gotten that list from Paul and would call him on Monday.

Things were moving rather quickly so John suggested that they take a hard look at where they were and to make any adjustments if needed. Dayton remarked that they needed to be sure that there is a clear understanding, with the owner, what is included in the sale of the business like the liquor supply.

The other big thing that they needed to discuss is if they would be taking salary from the business? John says no but Dayton says yes. Dayton loses a job with the purchase and John does have a job. John agrees that Dayton could continue to work as a bar tender part of the time and receive compensation for that time. He would be paid the same as John was being paid $1500 per month. So the problem was solved. Another question was posed by John. Is there a place at the pool hall where Maude could work or will she keep the job she has. Dayton replied for the time being Maude will continue at her present job.

John asked Dayton if he would talk to the attorney on Monday to see if all the forms were filled out to get the tax number and the registration of the name of the business. Maude was making dinner so she asked if John could stay and he said yes. And so another positive week has gone.

CHAPTER THIRTY THREE

John awoke at 7:30 on Sunday and had a cup of coffee to get him going. He would make it to Church for the 9:00 service and after that he would work on the proposal to be sent to potential Limited Partners. At 8:30 his phone rang and it was Sarah from the office. She called to invite him to have brunch with she and Judy. He was somewhat taken back by the invite but accepted the invitation. Sarah set the time for 11:30 and gave him directions to the restaurant. What a pleasant surprise. He would dress casually for the lunch. After thinking about it for a while, he knew that both ladies were single and was this invitation a date or just business?

They all arrived at about the same time. The ladies were dressed casually but to the"nines" Extremely attractive thought John. When the waiter approached them Judy said three Mimosas. John was ok with the choice.

Judy said that this get together was a way of making the relationship more binding in a casual sense. They both were very happy that John was working with them and they wanted to show their appreciation. John thought that the explanation was plausible and he expressed his thanks and hoped the relationship would be productive for all parties. The Mimosas came and all thoroughly enjoyed them. They then placed their orders. The ladies both ordered Eggs Benedict and John ordered scrambled eggs and smoked salmon(LOX) and a bagel with cream cheese.

They all drank coffee which was rich and smelled divine Judy inquired about John's experience at his former position at a brokerage firm in Dallas. John responded by saying it was just for a short time and he opted to resign to take advantage of the opportunity that brought him to Windsor. That opportunity was to build a series of purchases of bars and pool halls in Windsor with his partner, Dayton Hudson. This was being done as a General Partnership with the inclusion of Limited Partners along the way. They had just made their first purchase- Plummer's pool hall. It would be renamed Dayton Hudson. The business of the pool hall would not interfere with his job at Royal Bank. By the way the name of the Partnership was PHB Company.

The ladies seemed fascinated by John's remarks about the Partnership and expressed an interest in investing as Limited Partners. John said he would send them a ProForma as soon as it was ready. The brunch was delightful and they said their good byes and that they would see each other on Monday. John headed back to his apartment to work on the ProForma.

CHAPTER THIRTY FOUR

ohn arrived at his apartment and was ready to write the ProForma. but he first reflected on the brunch he had just enjoyed. It was apparent to him that Sarah was more aggressive than Judy as she did most of the talking. Was that meaningful or just his imagination?

John put on his "thinking cap" and started to work on the ProForma. First at the top of the page would be a picture of Plummer's Pool Hall The next section would be a description of the General Partners. " The General Partners would be John Drake who has had a great deal of experience in Finance in Dallas Texas and Dayton Hudson, a former professional Hockey player with the Dallas Avengers and the Toronto Maple Leafs"

The next section would be about the solicitation of Limited Partners. "The Limited Partners would produce the infusion of money into the partnership to be used for future purchases of bars and pool halls.

The next section would be about the purpose of The Partnership." The purpose of the Partnership is to purchase a series of bars and pool halls in Windsor Ontario over time".

The next section would be about the current and future Finances of the Partnership. The two General Partners have each put $30,000 into the Partnership. A loan has been obtained from the First National Bank of Windsor Ontario in the amount of $60,000. A sum of money, yet to be announced,would be the investments of the Limited Partners.

The next section would be about potential appreciation to General Partners and Limited Partners. The Limited Partners will be paid 4% annual interest on their investment paid quarterly. The General Partners will not receive any remuneration until an annual profit of $60,000 has been reached. They will not be paid any salary at this time as a General Partner but Dayton will get a salary as an employee. The Limited Partners will share in the profitability of the Partnership after an annual profit of $60,000 has been obtained to be paid after the General Partners are paid.

The next section would be about current events. "The Purchase of Plummers Pool Hall, in the amount of $100,000 has closed and the occupancy will happen within the next few days' The pool hall will be renamed Dayton Hudson. The solicitation of potential Limited Partners will happen in a few days. The minimum investment of the Limited Partners will be $5,000.

The next section will be the address of the Partnership and the phone number of the Partnership. The address will be the address of John Drake and his phone number.

John will bring this document to Dayton on Sunday to get his approval and then have it printed for delivery to John's and Dayton's lists. This could be done within the next week.

John felt that the document was good and hoped for a great reception from the potential partners. It was early evening when John completed writing the ProForma document. He did not feel like eating at home so he drove to the diner. After dinner he came home, watched a few TV shows and went to bed and reminded himself to call Dayton to bring the ProForma document to him on Sunday.

CHAPTER THIRTY FIVE

ohn called Dayton before going to Church and said they could meet at 10:30 at his apartment. It was ok with Dayton. John decided he would go to Sunday School at 10AM so he called Dayton and changed the time to 11:30. He told Dayton that he would bring sub sandwiches for lunch if Maude would brew some iced tea. He took their order and went off to Church. He enjoyed Church especially Sunday School where he met a bunch of folks The Class was about the study of the Bible and they were studying the Book of Mathew. He learned a lot. He stopped at a Subway and bought three Subs and some chips and headed to Dayton's.

Everyone seemed to enjoy their lunch which they ate prior to going over the ProForma. Dayton told John that he had finished preparing his list of potential Limited Partners and John hoped to have his list ready by Tuesday.

John gave Dayton a copy of the ProForma. He took about 15 minutes to read it before commenting on it. Dayton said it turned out very well except for one item. He said he would put the purpose of the Partnership before the item of Limited Partners. John thought that was a splendid idea. He asked Dayton if he could take several pictures of the pool hall tomorrow and take it all to the printers. We should use high grade paper for the ProForma and to purchase high grade envelopes with BPH on the letterhead and the top of the envelope.

Great thinking said Dayton. Both opined that things were moving along well and they were looking forward to the closing. John also asked Dayton if he would discuss the several matters John talked about the info about the employees etc and to be sure everything was included in the sale with the owner. Who was going to address the envelopes? Dayton said that Maude had an excellent writing skill so John would get his list to her as soon as he finished it. They decided to quit for the day. It was now 1PM and John wanted to go see the Junior Hockey game that started at 1:30. Did Dayton want to go? Dayton declined and said maybe another day and so John said goodbye.

He made it to the game on time and got a really good seat. The Hockey was good but not as good as the NHL but he enjoyed it anyway. The game was over at 4:30. John was not hungry so he went back to his apartment and decided to have soup and a sandwich for dinner. Tomorrow begins another week which he hoped would be eventful.

CHAPTER THIRTY SIX

Tomorrow came rather quickly for John He did not get a good night sleep because he was thinking about all the stuff that has to happen during the week. When he breaks for lunch he will call Paul to find out where the info is on all the names he gave him. He thought he would thank Sarah and Judy again for the brunch they treated him to.

He needed to talk to Dayton sometime late in the day to see how he made out with all the jobs he had to deal with especially with the owner and with the printer. Of course the first order of business is to close on the Pool Hall. When he talks to Dayton he needs to ask him to call the Title Company to see where the closing stands We need to be ready to send out the invitations as soon as the deal has closed.

Do we know who is going to build a new sign and who is going to hang it? All these things are important and we need to be prepared and not waste any time. John has concerns about a lot of things that Dayton has to deal with. He knows that Dayton has a lot on his plate but at this time that is the way it is. He has to rely on Dayton to be proactive.

It is important to John that he continues to have a good relationship with Sarah and Judy, because he needs and wants to keep his job. When he saw the ladies this morning he would thank them again for the brunch and hoped they could do it again to continue to cement the relationship.

It was lunch time and John had brought lunch with him. He hurried to eat so he would have time to call Paul. Paul answered his phone after the first ring. John asked him about the names as he allowed how important they were to the Partnership. Paul said they would go into today's mail with FedEx. John thanked him for getting it done He told Paul that the closing on the Pool Hall would happen in a few days and then the fun would begin. He would keep Paul up to date on the progress of signing up Limited Partners.

Later in the Dayton called and gave John a heads up on his tasks for today. The attorney has filed the necessary paper work to get the tax id and the designation of the name of the Partnership. He also said that the paper and the envelopes had been decided on and the photographs of the Pool Hall had been taken and will be incorporated into the letter going out to prospective Partners. The printing will be ready tomorrow. He had not yet reached Mr. Plummer but he will keep on trying. John told Dayton that his list would be available tomorrow. Has Dayton found someone to build the new sign and someone to hang it? Dayton replied that he would see to it over the next 24 hours. Would he please call the Title Company to find out when the closing would be. John thanked him for all the good work he has been doing and said they should talk this evening to touch base with the things on the agenda. Dayton said that he felt that things were proceeding in relatively good speed and that he would continue to work on the things that were still up in the air but he needed to go to work soon.

Sarah and Judy seemed to be in a very good mood this morning and he wondered that it was because of the Brunch on Sunday? He did thank them again for the wonderful Brunch.

CHAPTER THIRTY SEVEN

arah and Judy kept John very busy during the afternoon with new account paper work and various other tasks. The day moved quickly and it was now 4PM. Sarah asked me to look into a complaint from one of her clients about the price the client received on a stock transaction. The client thought he should have been filled at a lower price. John called the department which handles trades on the New York Stock Exchange and they told her they would look into the complaint.

It was now 5PM and time to leave. He called Dayton at the Pool Hall to see when they could meet at Dayton's apartment. Dayton said it could not be until 9PM and that was ok with John as it would be a short meeting. John left the office and headed home. He was not very hungry so he made two chicken sandwiches which he ate at 7PM. He watched TV until 8:30 and left home to go see Dayton. He wished that he had the list of potential Partners but that would be tomorrow.

Dayton showed John a schematic of what the letter to potential Partners would look like and the stationary the printer would use. The initials BPH and the picture of the Pool Hall were present on the schematic. John was very pleased with the choices that Dayton had made. Dayton went on to say that he was not able to reach Mr. Plummer and would try again tomorrow. He would find a way to reach him.

Maude had baked an Apple pie so she offered both John and Dayton a piece with a scoop of Vanilla ice cream on top. They both said of course They all enjoyed the dessert. It was John's feeling that all of the main concerns would be taken care of by the end of the week especially the mailings of the ProForma to prospective Partners. They had no idea what the response would be and, yet, they were optimistic about the results. They would like to have subscriptions of over $100,000 so they could look to buy another property which Dayton felt would be a bar that he has scoped out. In fact he had two bars on his list. The evening closed on a positive note.

CHAPTER THIRTY EIGHT

ayton called early in the morning to tell John that he had talked to the owner and that everything is included. He did have a computer and a printer and mouse and screen which he is taking with him so we need to buy all that stuff John said he would buy all of that on the way home today. Dayton went on to say that he has taken care of the new sign and someone to install it. John said "I have forgotten. Did the attorney get the id and name squared away'? "Yes he did and by the way the closing is set for Friday at 2PM "said Dayton. John also asked Dayton to check with the owner to see if he has any kind of list of customers that we could use. " I will pick up the printing in a few hours and the sign will be ready tomorrow" said Dayton.

John said that he told the manager of his apartment complex to look out for the package from FedEx. "If it was delivered today he would bring it to Dayton this evening" said John. John was very much satisfied that Dayton had done such a good job on following up on the outstanding concerns. John was aware that he was taking away from his job the conversation with Dayton but the ladies didn't seem to be concerned.

The afternoon at work was very busy for John and he managed to take care of all that he had to do so he could leave at 5PM. H e did leave at 5PM and stopped at the electronics store to purchase the computer, printer et al. When he arrived at home the FedEx package was leaning against his front door. He opened it and all of the names had addresses next to them. He got back in his car after calling Maude to be sure she was home to accept the package.

Maude could begin addressing the envelopes awaiting Dayton's bringing home the stationary. Dayton left early to bring home the stationary and the new sign which would be installed after the closing. Dayton was getting "goose bumps" as he knew the ProForma letters would be in the mail the next day. It really was happening.

John arrived at 7PM and Dayton was there to greet him. Maude showed John that she has already addressed some of the envelopes and that she could finish doing all that evening. Together there were over 50 names on the two list. John asked Dayton to give him 12 copies of the ProForma plus envelopes that he could use to supplement the ones that Maude was working on. He would give one to Judy and Sarah tomorrow plus sending ones to his family. It was pretty late by the time John left to go home.

     PHILIP STEPHENS

CHAPTER THIRTY NINE

John awoke earlier than usual the next morning. He thought it was because he was so excited about the mailing that would take place today. He hoped that Dayton had purchased stamps. John did not know if you used different Canadian stamps for letters sent to the US. Probably Dayton knew what to do. John needed to purchase some stamps also so he could mail ProFormas to his family. Maybe there was a post office nearby his office. He would ask the Operations Manager when he gets to work.

John would quietly give the ProFoma to Judy and Sarah. He thought about giving one to the Office Manager but he thought he would ask the ladies if they thought it would be ok. If he did he would need to tell him that being a General Partner would not interfere with his job and he would not offer it to any of the company's clients.

When he gave the ProForma to the ladies he asked about giving one to the Manager and they thought not to They said that under no conditions would they recommend this Partnership to any of their clients but maybe to family members and possibly friends. They thought it would be a good investment.

Dayton forgot to buy stamps so the first thing he did was to go to the post office to buy them. He would ask if there was a special stamp for letters to the US. The answer was there was not. Maude and Dayton put the stamps on the 50 or so ProFormas that were ready to go out and took them to the Post Office. They were so excited that they almost couldn't stand it.

Dayton thought that a celebration was called for and he would call John to invite him to such a celebration. They made a date to meet at Dayton's favorite restaurant, The French Connection at 6PM. Dayton called ahead to have the restaurant put a bottle of Champagne on ice for that evenings meal. Dayton did find out from Mr. Plummer that he had such a list of his best customers so Dayton picked the list up on his way home. He also called the printer to have 50 more copies of the ProForma plus envelopes printed up as he figured they would need them.

They met for dinner and enjoyed the champagne with lots of cheer at their table. Not being concerned about the closing, they all understood that the game is on The closing would happen without any problems. The meal was fabulous better than Dayton had expected. The bill was for over $100 but it was worth it. They all left the restaurant a bit tipsy to make their way home. Hugs and kisses were spread around.

CHAPTER FORTY

There were several things John needed to do. One was to have Dayton order 100 sheets of stationary with the Partnership's initials at the top of the page and 100 envelopes with their initials at the upper left corner. They would need them to send confirmation of sale back to the new Limited Partners. The second thing they would need is a ledger book for simple accounting with entrees either money in and money out. It did not have to be anything more complicated. They would also need several bags to place the days receipts in to take to the Bank When Dayton gets the check on Thursday from the Bank he can get some deposit bags. On the way home from the office today John needed to go to Barnes and Nobles to buy the ledger. John would call the Bank to have them print a three hole binder check book for the Partnership knowing that the first checks would be temporary as the three hole binder has to be printed. All of this John thought of before his first cup of coffee.

When John got to the office the ladies presented John with checks made out to BPH Partnership in the amount of $10,000 each. The first purchases for the Partnership. John was effusive in his thank you to the ladies. He called Dayton immediately to give him the good news. John thought he couldn't wait to get the stationary to write the official confirmation to the ladies. This was a good sign that they would get a bunch of positive responses from the new Limited Partners. How cool was that. At lunch time he called the Bank to ask them to give Dayton some temporary Partnership checks while ordering permanent three hole binder checks. John will pick them up on Friday morning when he gets the check for $60,000 which is the loan amount. Dayton will deposit the $60,000 in their Partnership account and use one of the temporary checks to write the check for $100,000 to be given to Mr. Plummer at the closing.

The closing is scheduled for 11AM on Friday. Dayton will be there representing the Partnership but John will be at work. They had decided to spend all day Saturday and Sunday setting up the office getting rid of stuff they don't need. John would ask Dayton to have the sign put up shortly after the closing and Dayton would take over the management of the Pool Hall at that time. Lots to do over the next few days. John went to Barnes and Noble after work and purchased the Ledger book which he will bring to the Pool Hall on Friday after work. The first entry will be the Purchase of the Pool Hall for $100,000 and that will be on the "money going out" side of the ledger.

CHAPTER FORTY ONE

Dayton told John that he, being the Manager of the Pool Hall, it was necessary to Appoint an Assistant Manager. His choice would be the first shift bartender, Timothy Gagne. They would raise his salary by ten %. A good part of Timothy's income does come from tips. All of the employees, of which there are only a few, get paid every week on Friday. There are two guys that manage the Pool tables setting players up at specific tables and getting the money for the rental of the table which is paid for on an hourly basis. These two guys are very important as they control the income from the tables. Sometimes they get tips from the patrons.

It will be Dayton's responsibility to count the money in the cash register every evening after closing and putting the days proceeds into a Bank deposit bag and entering that amount in the ledger book on the side of money in. He would drive to the Bank and place the deposit bag into the deposit slot He would also count the money left in the register and leave the amount for Timothy to double check the next morning.

Today was Friday and the closing would happen in a few hours. John was on pins and needles waiting to hear from Dayton that all was ok. At 11:30 Dayton called and said "We own a Pool Hall". Dayton went on to say that he was off to the Pool Hall to get the new sign installed and tend bar for the rest of the day. He would count the money in the register and make their first deposit in the Bank. Everything from now on belonged to the Partnership. It was a glorious beginning.

John told Dayton that he would be at the Pool Hall at 9AM tomorrow to begin the restructuring of the office and, of course, to see the first cash entry in the ledger book that he brought with him. They were on their way. Dayton would be at the Pool Hall at 8AM to welcome the employees which included the two guys who run the tables and the other guy who keeps things clean and spic and spam. Timothy would show up at 8:30 ready to open the bar at 9AM. Maude came with Dayton to help with setting up the office.

The employees were used to be paid on Friday but since the closing took place on Friday Mr. Plummer paid them on Friday morning for the past week which ended on Thursday. The next check to the employees would be the responsibility of BPH would be next Friday for the week beginning yesterday and ending next Thursday.

CHAPTER FORTY TWO

John was up early today being Saturday. He would be at the Pool Hall to help in the setting up the office. He would bring the computer and printer to the office and set it up. While waiting for the coffee to brew his phone rang and it was his brother calling from his home in Florida. He called to see if the closing had taken place. John replied that everything was done and they now owned their first Pool Hall. Pete went on to say that he was sending him a check for $10,000 for his position as a Limited Partner. He also said that their parents were also sending him a check for $10,000. John was excited to hear that news and expressed his thanks. Pete told him that things were going well for him at Merrill. He would be producing around $300,000 in commissions for the year. They both said love you and hung up.

They had a total of $40,000 in Limited Partner sign ups. They were well on their way to the goal of $100,000 and he knew Dayton would be happy. Since the ProForma had just been sent out a few days ago, he didn't expect more money coming in just yet.

When John arrived at the Pool Hall he was glad to see the new sign up on the building. They were really in business now. The first thing he did was to set up the computer system and the printer. Both Dayton and Maude were already there and he told Dayton that the total money from Limited Partners was $40,000. They were going through the paper work in the files getting rid of a lot of stuff. Dayton had already entered in the ledger the receipts from Friday. The purchase had already been entered by John. They had a brief meeting with the staff introducing themselves to the group. The also said that with help of the staff the revenue will increase over time. The doors to the Pool Hall were opened at 9:00 and the staff took their places. Dayton was behind the bar while Maude and John continued to set up the office mainly to get rid of papers that were no longer needed. Dayton told Timothy about his new position and that he was getting a 10% increase in salary. Tim was very pleased.

John had developed a few marketing plans to get them started. He would run an ad celebrating new management and also to advertise that starting on Monday, a week from next Monday, all women accompanied by a guy would get a free beer and that would be a permanent deal on Mondays. They would use the list that Mr. Plummer gave Dayton to announce the new ownership and reveal the free beer promotion. Dayton would go to the printer on Monday and have the letters printed up and then mail the letters. Dayton thought it was a great idea and supported it. By 10:30 Maude and John had finished setting up the office. The ledger book was in special place that all could see. On Friday, the day before, Dayton notified the power company and the phone company about the change of ownership. John picked up the extra ProForma letters and envelopes that he asked Dayton to have printed up. He would use the list that Mr. Plummer had of his best customers. John wished everyone well and took off to his apartment.

Today was Saturday and Paul would not be in the office so he called him at home. He told Paul about the closing and the new sign "Dayton Hudson". He had sent a ProForma letter to Paul so he asked him if he was going to be a Limited Partner. Paul said yes and he would put a check in the mail today. John thanked him and said he would keep in touch.

     PHILIP STEPHENS

CHAPTER FORTY THREE

John bought a newspaper on his way home and he read the paper while having another cup of coffee. The advertisement on the free beer promotion would be in Sunday's paper. John was certain that it would be well received. The restaurant reminded him of the Deli News etc.

His phone rang and it was Sarah wanting to know if they all could meet for brunch tomorrow. John was pleased to hear from her and said he could, meet after Church and Sunday School, at 11:30 at the same place they had met before. John was looking forward to seeing them on Sunday. It seemed a bit odd that they would make a date for brunch so soon after their last meeting for brunch.

John decided to make another drive around town especially to look at more neighborhoods of single family homes. In the back of his mind he thought that eventually he would like to move into his own home and leave the apartment but that was in the future.

On his last trip around town he drove by a delicatessen and told himself that he would stop there for lunch one day. So today was the day. The restaurant reminded him of the.

Deli News delicatessen in Richardson on the outskirts of Dallas. He ordered a huge pastrami sandwich with potato salad and a diet cream soda. It made him a bit homesick for Dallas while enjoying his lunch.

After lunch he made his way to several single family homes neighborhood. One particular neighborhood caught his eye. There was a large park in the area and a few strip shopping centers. He liked the style of houses and thought he would take another look at this area when he was ready to buy a home.

He got home at about 3PM and was a bit tired so he decided to take a short nap. The short nap was not so short. It was 3 hours when he awoke at 6PM. He looked at the TV schedule in the paper he had purchased on the way home. He noticed that there was a Toronto Maple Leafs game at 7PM so he put a TV dinner into the microwave and ate the food and finished right ay 7PM. The game was a good one going into overtime when the Leafs scored in the first two minutes to win the game. He reminisced after the game about the games back in Dallas with the Dallas Avengers and Dayton's play.

CHAPTER FORTY FOUR

A cup or two of coffee before going to Church and Sunday School. They were still on the Book of Matthew. For some reason he remembered as a little kid that the Book of Matthew was taught in Sunday School but he could not remember anything from kids Sunday School about Matthew.

He got to the restaurant on time and Sarah was waiting for him. No Judy present. Sarah said that Judy was not feeling well and decided not to come. What was the truth.? He would check it out with Judy tomorrow. John would have Sarah all to himself and take advantage of the time together. He asked Sarah about her growing up. Sarah said she grew up in Sudbury Ontario one of three girls she being the youngest. She was pretty much considered to be a "tomboy" as a youngster participating in basketball and track. Her skills were evident in her track experience having been the number one quarter miler in Canada. It got her a scholarship to College in Montreal. She graduated third in her class at McGill University. While at McGill she became interested in finance and graduated with a BS in Business. Royal Bank of Canada visited her campus and they offered her a job as a Financial Consultant which she accepted. It has been 5 years since she began her job at RBC and she has loved every bit of the time she has been in Windsor. She believes she has been very successful as a Consultant and has a really good book of clients.

It was John's time to share. He grew up in Brooklyn New York and was very active in the three major sports; Basketball, Football and Baseball. However his favorite sport was Street Roller Hockey. He asked Sarah if they played Roller Hockey in Canada? Sarah said she did not think so. John continued saying he wanted to play Ice Hockey but could not afford the cost of equipment.

He went away to Prep School in Pennsylvania and then to The Wharton School of Finance and Commerce. He got married at the age of 21 but the marriage lasted 8 years during which time he spent as a broker at Merrill Lynch in Dallas Texas. One of his clients was Dayton Hudson who was playing minor league hockey in Dallas with the farm team of Toronto Maple Leafs. They became good friends. When Dayton decided to move back to Windsor where he grew up and decided to start his own business. John decided to quit Merrill and move to Canada as a single man and go into Partnership with Dayton and the rest is history.

John asked Sarah if she had been married to which she answered no but she had a boyfriend in College but that ended some time ago. She doesn't date that much and John said that was good. He confessed that he has grown to be a bit smitten with Sarah and would like to date her. It would have to be on the sly as it would not be a good idea for that relationship to get around for business reasons. Sarah's response was positive and so it began. They parted with a hug although John thought about kissing her but thought the better of it.

When John got home he found the list of Mr. Plummer's best clients and addressed envelopes to them containing the announcement of the new ownership plus the beer promotion. He would pick up stamps tomorrow and mail them. He watched a bit of TV and had a sandwich before going to bed. He wanted to call Sarah but did not have her phone number. He would see to that tomorrow.

          PHILIP STEPHENS

CHAPTER FORTY FIVE

When John got to work he told Judy that he was sorry that she did not come to brunch on Sunday. Her response was that she was not invited. It was clear now that Sarah had planned it that way. Apparently Judy was ok with that and no doubt Sarah clued in Judy about the outcome of the brunch with John. Both John and Sarah had to be careful at work not acting too cozy with each other. It would be difficult but not impossible.

He needed to get stamps at lunchtime to mail the beer promotion and the new ownership announcement. He checked with Dayton right before lunch to see what was going on. Dayton said that 6 of the tables were being used but no one was in the bar area. He also said that all the guys are working hard and Tim is very happy with his new responsibility and the 10% raise.

John was very pleased that he had a relationship going forward with Sarah. Who knows where the relationship would end up? One could only speculate. When John had a moment he asked Sarah for her phone number which she gave him when no one was looking, How fortunate John was to be involved with a beauty like Sarah. On some level he tries to compare Jo to Sarah but found that very difficult.

He couldn't wait till he got home today to see if there were any more responses to the Limited Partner mailing. Perhaps it is too soon for there to be any. He would be sending confirmations out to Pete, his parents,

Sarah and Judy when he got home. At lunch he went to the post office and bought a bunch of stamps as they would be needed. He needed to draft a confirmation letter to be used for the first times today.

He heard from Pete today about his pending engagement to his future wife Barbara. He sounded joyous. John asked when would the wedding be and Pete answered they had not set a date. How did they meet asked John? They met at the local gym and have been dating for abut 6 months Barbara was a CPA and worked for Peat Marwick. John was very happy for Pete and told Pete he would call him this evening to get more information on his engagement.

CHAPTER FORTY SIX

When John got home from work, he checked the mailbox and there was none but John didn't expect any as it was too soon. The next thing he did was to call Sarah. She answered on the 2nd ring. It was as if John couldn't wait to talk to her. He told her that he couldn't stop staring at her during the day at work. He needed to stop that because if people were looking it would become obvious that there was something going on. He also said that he didn't think they should meet during the week and only date on the weekends. They had to find places where they could meet. They spoke for about an hour and, the more they talked, the more infatuated John felt about Sarah. They both said see you tomorrow.

His next phone call was to Pete. Pete talked a lot about his relationship with Barbara and how it was love a first site for both of them. Barbara was a native New Yorker but her family moved to Florida when she was 12. She went to University of Miami and studied accounting and was offered a job with Peat Marwick after graduation. She was an athlete in College lettering 4 years at volley ball. He was so fortunate to meet her and build the relationship. John told Pete that things were going well at his job and the Partnership. He shared about the beer promotion and Pete thought that was a great idea. The subject of Sarah came up and John was "over the moon" with that relationship. He shared with Pete how the relationship with Sarah began and how it blossomed. They said their goodbyes.

He next called his parents to thank them for the check for the Limited Partnership even though he had not gotten it yet. His Dad said the check was in the mail. He also shared about his new relationship with a lady named Sarah and he thought that he was in love. His Mom thought that it was a good thing. John was enjoying his new job and the Partnership was doing well.

Time was getting away from John so he decided to go to the diner to eat dinner. It was pretty crowded so he ate at the counter. The food was always good there. After supper he came back home and started addressing the envelopes to Mr. Plummer's list regarding the new ownership and the beer promotion. He stamped all of them and went to bed and would mail them on his way to work tomorrow.

CHAPTER FORTY SEVEN

The next day John called Dayton to check of the proceeds from Monday. Dayton said they were excellent and the system they were using to keep track of the proceeds and the nightly deposits was working well. John thought that he would stop by the Pool Hall on the way home from work. The day moved quickly and John was not staring at Sarah as much as he did the day before. Both Sarah and Judy were both busy putting in orders from their clients. The markets were up for the day so the orders were more than usual. Before John left for the day he asked Sarah if she wanted to go to dinner with him which was against the rules that John had stated a few days ago but they went anyway. He decided to postpone his going to the Pool Hall for another day. They decided to meet at the Delicatessen near John's apartment which would be a safe place to meet.

It was 5:30 before they both got to the restaurant. John said that this restaurant reminded him of one back in Dallas and it made him a bit homesick. This was the first time Sarah had eaten at the Delicatessen and she thoroughly enjoyed her dinner. They lingered there for about two hours talking about things they would like to do together. It was a lot of fun focusing on their relationship. John wanted to invite Sarah back to his apartment but though that it was too soon for sex so at 7:30 they hugged and kissed and it was a very good kiss and said goodbye and would see each other tomorrow. John's hormones were exploding but it was too soon to explore the possibility of sex.

John drove home with an empty feeling being without the company of Sarah. He needed to talk to Sarah about extending their relationship via sex. He felt comfortable in expressing his wishes. When he got home he took a cold shower which tamped down his hormones and that was a good thing. The Toronto Maple Leafs hockey game was on TV so he watched it and it took his mind off of Sarah. The game was over at 10PMand he was not tired so he watched a movie until 11:30 and went to sleep hoping to have a good dream about Sarah and himself. Unfortunately that didn't materialize.

He forgot to check the mailbox so he went to the mailbox and found 5 envelopes. One was from his parents. One was from Paul. One was from Pete for $5000. The other two were from Dayton list and they were for $5000. Each So the count is now $55,000. He needed to write confirmations to all of them.

CHAPTER FORTY EIGHT

When John got to the office on Thursday, he called Dayton to tell him that he received two more Partnerships from Dayton's list and the total was now $55,000. He would stop by after work to see how things were going and to tell him who the two additional Partnerships were. He would write confirmations tonight to all subscribers.

They were half way to their goal of $100,000 so it was time to think about their next purchase. Maybe they could visit the two bars on Saturday and make a choice. John was overjoyed that things were moving so quickly. This made him nervous and they should talk about maybe slowing things down a bit. Wait and see how the Pool Hall was doing before spending anymore money. It made perfect sense to John and he would share his thoughts with Dayton.

Somehow the Manager at Royal Bank of Canada found out that Sarah and Judy had purchased Limited Partnerships in John's General Partnership so he called John to his office to talk about it. John was scared that maybe he would lose his job. The conversation was very positive. In fact, would John give him a ProForma because he might invest also. John was relieved and, at the same time, glad that the Manager might invest. So he needed to remind himself to bring a copy of the ProForma to give to him tomorrow.

Judy wasn't feeling well so she left early. John asked Sarah if Judy was ok. Sarah allowed that Judy has migraine headaches from time to time and she needed to be in dark and quiet room which would be at her apartment.

It was 5PM and John left to go to the Pool Hall and to see Dayton. He gave Dayton the names of the two people that purchased Limited Partnerships. He then went to the ledger and entered the twp purchases of computer stuff, one for himself and one for the office. He looked at the entries of income for Monday, Tuesday and Wednesday. The totals, about $1000 Per day, were pleasing to John but he thought they were a bit below what the Pool Hall had taken in over the past year. He figured it was because folks needed to get used to the new ownership. The number will improve especially with the beer promotion happening next Monday.

John wanted to talk to Dayton about waiting to see how the Pool Hall does over the next month or so before deciding to make another purchase. They also needed to see how many Limited Partnerships were sold. Dayton was in agreement with John.

John had not talked to Dayton about his relationship with Sarah and the fact that she was an Account Executive in his office and that John worked for her. John proposed going on a double date on Friday night with Dayton and Maude. They decided to meet at the French Connection at 7 on Friday. Dayton approved. He would share that with Sarah on the phone tonight.

CHAPTER FORTY NINE

When John arrived home he went directly to the mailbox and found three replies on the Partnership. Two were from former clients of his for $5000 each and one from one off Dayton's list for $10,000. That brings the total to $75.000. Great total bringing them closer to $100,000.

He called Sarah and she was home. John discussed the conversation he had with Dayton, his partner. He thought it was about time for Sarah to meet him and his wife Maude so they decided to meet Friday night at 7Pm at the French Connection. Sarah thought it was a wonderful idea and she looked forward to meeting them.

Today is Friday and everyone was looking forward to meeting tonight at the French Connection. It was an opportunity for all to be on the same page and that is the success of the Partnership. Everyday's response from the potential Limited Partners will go a long way to moving the Partnership in the right direction. John was happy that Dayton agreed to wait for good results from the Pool Hall and from more people buying into the Partnership.

John called Dayton shortly after arriving at work to tell him That he received three more Limited Partners agreements. One was from your list and it was $10,000 and two were from my list and they totaled $10,000. The total now was $75,000. He has mailed confirmations to all who have subscribed.

Dayton said the receipts from Thursday were better than the previous days. They totaled $1500 which was a major improvement.

The day passed quickly. John told Sarah that he would pick her up at 6:30. They all arrived at the restaurant at the same time. Introductions were made and they all settled down to what they hoped to be a very cordial dinner. The waiter came and took the drink orders and the conversation was moving along at a good pace. The girls talked a lot about their jobs while Dayton and John spent the time listening to that conversation. John still had his rental car and decided to get a replacement vehicle tomorrow. He asked Sarah if she could go with him and she said of course.

John thought the dinner went well and all departed at around 9:30. John drove to Sarah's apartment and Sarah asked him to come in and John obliged. Sarah brewed some coffee and they shared a cup. John asked what Sarah thought about the dinner. The first thing she said was how much do you trust Dayton because I have a bad feeling about Dayton in that there was something about him that made me feel that he was untrustworthy. John was really surprised at her comments and said that he trusted him but he respected Sarah's opinion and would be watching Dayton's behavior.

They finished their coffee and John brought up the subject of their relationship. He said that he was all in on it and hoped that Sarah felt the same. Sarah showed her approval by kissing him really hard and John responded. So, John asked about the subject of taking another step forward in their relationship and that would be having sex. To his surprise Sarah said she was all for that. That doesn't mean that it had to happen that evening but it would be in play going forward. So they kissed some more and said good night a short time later and made a date to be together tomorrow evening. John left, and for the most part, felt that the dinner went well and the subject of sex was a home run. He also would consider Sarah's intuition about Dayton.

     PHILIP STEPHENS

CHAPTER FIFTY

John slept in on Saturday awakened at 9 and immediately called Sarah. He said he would pick her up at 10 to go car shopping. He had not checked his mailbox as it was late and he was tired last night. He got dressed and went to see if he had any mail. There were two pieces of mail both of which were from Limited Partner responses. He opened both envelopes and one was from his list for $5000 and one was from Dayton's list for $10,000. The total was now $90,000. He would call Dayton later in the day to give him the totals.

He drove to Sarah's apartment and rang her door bell. She let him in and asked him if he would like a cup of coffee which he did. John asked what she knew about car dealers in Windsor, She said there was a central location where there were many dealers. She bought her Buick SUV there. John wanted to lease a car as he might be able to take a tax deduction. They drove to that location and John saw that Sarah was right about the number of dealers there.

John had owned a Ford Expedition in Dallas but he was open for suggestions. They visited the Ford dealer and John liked the Ford Explorer and, after a bit of haggling, he leased the car. Both he and Sarah were pleased with his choice. John realized that he ought to get a Canadian driver's license so he would look into that next week. By that time it was 11:30 and John asked Sarah to recommend a place to go to for brunch.

She did and they headed that way after getting directions from Sarah. The restaurant was kind of in he country and it was a perfect setting.

They asked to be seated outside and they ordered Mimosas and told the waiter to give them some time to decide what to eat. The menu was huge but they lingered a while enjoying their Mimosas. They held hands for a while and both were happy to be together. They even stole a kiss while waiting to order. It appeared that they were both in love. They enjoyed their food but especially the environment and they ate slowly happy to be in that setting. They stayed at the restaurant until 1Pm and John wanted to show Sarah the homes he had looked at recently. He wanted to get Sarah's opinion of the neighborhood as he was thinking of buying a home there.

They drove around the area for about 45 minutes and saw a few homes for sale. Sarah liked neighborhood and said if she wanted to buy a house this would be a perfect area to live in. It was close to shopping and she had heard that the school system was excellent. John filed her comments in his head hoping that it would be relevant in the near future.

Perhaps this would be the day they had sex so John said he needed to pick up a few things at the drug store so they stopped at the first one they saw. John went in alone while Sarah waited in the car. John purchased condoms because he didn't want to chance Sarah becoming pregnant. They drove back to Sarah's apartment and went inside, The time was perfect. They began kissing and before long they both took each others clothes off in a frenzy. John said it had been a while since he had sex and so did Sarah so they took their time enjoying each others bodies. It was an amazing experience for both of them as they were very compatible sexually. After things had reached a climax they lay there in each others arms again enjoying each other bodies. They kissed for a while and they decided to shower with each other. That was a big turn on for both of them examining each others bodies and so they had sex again for the 2nd

     PHILIP STEPHENS

time. They were both exhausted so they lay there again beside each other. John remarked that this sex thing could become a habit. Sarah laughed at John's comment.

The time had moved fast and it was now 6Pm so they decided to order pizza for dinner. It has been a perfectly wonderful day all around. They enjoyed the pizza. John wanted to watch the Maple Leafs on TV so he asked Sarah if that was ok and she said yes. It was 10PM when the game was over and they were both tired so they kissed and John said goodbye and said they would see each other on Monday.

John was in heaven, so to speak, on his way home. He did remember to check the mailbox but it was empty. He called Dayton to tell him that the total was now $90000 and then he hit the hay earlier than usual.

CHAPTER FIFTY ONE

When John leased the car in Dallas they told him whereto bring the car in Windsor when he was ready to turn it in. So he got up early on Monday, called the car rental place to get directions and drove to that location. He paid the bill and asked if they would drive him back to his apartment so he could drive his new car to work. He called Sarah at 7:30 at home and told her he would be late to work because he had to turn in his rental car.

He finally arrived at work at 8:30. He told Sarah and Judy that he was sorry to be late but he had to turn his rental car in. He called Dayton and asked how business was over the weekend. Dayton said they averaged $2500 per day over the weekend. Dayton went on to say that he needed to buy more beer and liquor from the wholesale distributor. John said he would drop by the Pool Hall after work today to look at the ledger book. Today was the day when the beer promotion was to start and he hoped it would be successful.

John was happy at his job and thought he should get a raise based on the help he had been to Sarah and Judy so he would broach that subject to the ladies since they had to approve the raise when going to the manager. They did that and the manager called John into his office to tell him that he approved a raise of 10% which John really appreciated.

John called the Motor Vehicle place in Windsor to ask about getting a Canadian driver's license. They told him that if he had a up to date

US license they would issue him a Canadian license. They were open on Saturdays so John planned to go there next Saturday'

Fall was approaching and the weather was getting cooler. John needed to purchase a winter coat so he thought he would go to the department store after work today and left work at 5PM and went to the store to buy one. Since they got their share of snow in the winter in Windsor, he also bought a pair of boots and a scarf. While there at the store he saw a rather nice looking sweater so he purchased that also.

After leaving the store he headed for the Pool Hall. When he got there he checked the proceeds in the ledger book and everything looked ok, He asked Dayton to let him know when he got the monthly bank statement so he could check the ledger book versus what the bank says was deposited. Just checking up on Dayton. The Hall was crowded which he hoped was because of the beer promotion. He would find out from Dayton the revenue for Monday.

CHAPTER FIFTY TWO

It was Tuesday and John was at work at 7:45. He said hi to everyone that was there including Judy and Sarah. Judy asked him to type a few letters for her which he did in no time at all. Did she want them mailed or faxed? Judy gave him the fax numbers which he used immediately. Judy said thank you. John asked her how her migraine headaches were doing and she replied about the same.

He called Dayton at 9:15 to inquire about the take for Monday. Dayton said about $3100 which he thought was good. John decided to call Mr. Plummer. He asked Mr. Plummer what was the average take on weekdays and the weekend for the Pool Hall. He replied about $3000 on weekdays and $4000 on the weekend. John was shocked to hear the numbers being as high as they were. He told Mr. Plummer that his numbers were about 20% or so less and did he have any idea why that was so. Mr. Plummer said that it was probably due to the new ownership with people not being sure as yet as to the quality of care by the new owners. John was not buying that for a minute.

How was John going to deal with that? He called Dayton and said he wanted to come by after work to discuss a few things with him. Dayton said come ahead. John arrived at 5:30 and got together with Dayton in the office. He asked Dayton if he had any idea why the revenue was about 20% less per week than it was when Plummer owned the Pool Hall. Dayton came up with the same idea that Mr. Plummer had given

       PHILIP STEPHENS

John. John said he didn't believe that was the reason so he decided to send a questionnaire to the list of Plummer's best clients. He would make up that questionnaire over the next few days. He had the list at his apartment and he needed some additional stationary to use for that questionnaire.

John was getting suspicious of the reason for the drop in revenue and was bound and determined to find the answer. Was somebody skimming the take? He hoped this was not the case. The only people that could pull that off were the bar tenders, Tim and Dayton. He did not know Tim except he had been there for several years and there apparently was no problem with Tim so that left Dayton.

John prepared the questionnaire asking if they were still coming to the Pool Hall and, if not, why were they not coming. He asked them to reply by phone at his apartment phone number between 6PM and 9PM. He would mail them tomorrow as he had sufficient stamps with him.

CHAPTER FIFTY THREE

He called Sarah after addressing the questionnaire and told her about the 20% drop in revenue. Her first thought was the same as Plummer and Dayton thoughts were but almost immediately she said she did not believe that was the reason. For sure John needed to get to the bottom of the problem and she would help if needed.

John could not sleep that night worrying about the numbers. Maybe Sarah was right about not trusting Dayton but he felt that it is difficult to believe but at this point anything is possible.

He arose at 7Am and went through his usual routine before going to work. He had forgotten to check his mailbox yesterday so before he left he checked it. There was just one reply in there for $5000 from one of Dayton's list which brought the total to $95,000.

He worried all day about the money and could not concentrate. Sarah noticed that John was not himself so she told him to cool it and everything would be settled one way or the other. John tried to act normally but it was difficult. He could not wait for the day to be over so he could call Dayton to check on Wednesday's receipts. Dayton said that the take was $2300. John said he had hoped that the take would be back to normalcy but that was not the case.

Maybe Dayton, if he is guilty, had gotten a clue that I am investigating the shortfall. So lets give it a couple of more weeks and see if there is a upward change. Today is Thursday so give it about 10 days.

John decided to make several visits to the Pool Hall over the next 10 days to alert Dayton that he is checking up on the numbers. He hoped to get some good reply to the questionnaire he sent out. That would give him more information on the shortfall.

John is having a hard time seeing Sarah everyday but not able to be with her or even stare at her. Should they make the relationship obvious to all? What would the manager say? The manager should not care if there is no change in the work habits of either John or Sarah. He needs to have a conversation with Sarah ASAP. He would call Sarah at home this evening to discuss the matter.

John decided to make a trip to the Pool Hall after work to check the ledger. It would be a surprise visit as he usually calls Dayton before showing up. When he arrived he asked Dayton if the Bank statement had showed up and Dayton said no. John checked the register and it seemed ok so John went home.

There were two more responses to the Limited Partner ProForma one from John's list for $5000 and one from Dayton's list for $5000 bringing the total to $105,000. Hooray they met their goal so he called Dayton to give him the good news. Dayton did not seem overly excited about the news which bothered John.

CHAPTER FIFTY FOUR

John wanted to stay home tonight expecting replies to the questionnaire so he ate a TV dinner. He decided to call Paul and get his take on the shortfall. He gave Paul all the info he had including the questionnaire he sent out with no replies as yet. Paul never had a lot of contact with Dayton so he had no comment on Dayton as a person. However, he did say that things looked suspicious and John was doing what was necessary to get to the bottom of the problem. He went on to say that some time needed to go by before John might have a better sense of what might be going on. Perhaps eventually John would have to confront Dayton which would be a difficult thing to do.

John thanked Paul for his take on the problem and asked him to call if he had other ideas. There were two calls that came in while John was talking to Paul so he returned both calls. The response to the questionnaire was the same, They said that they have continued to frequent the Pool Hall and will continue to do so. They wished John good luck.

He then called Sarah to tell her what Paul had said and also the two responses he got from the questionnaire. Sarah had a similar response as Paul had that probably he might have to confront Dayton after he looks at the bank statement and got more responses to the questionnaire. They made a date to meet for dinner tomorrow evening. John would pick her up at 7PM and they could decide where to eat. He decided to wait until tomorrow evening to talk about the secrecy or non secrecy of their relationship.

After getting off the phone he received two more responses to the questionnaire and they were carbon copies of the other responses. This was good in one sense but also bad in another sense as it seems to be ruling out that the good clients were not coming back. Bummer. He hated the thought of having to confront his friend and business partner but it was too soon to contemplate that action. There were two more calls that evening regarding the questionnaire and, again, the response was the same. He watched a bit of TV to get his mind off the problem and went to sleep at about 10:30

CHAPTER FIFTY FIVE

It was Friday and another week was coming to a close. He tried to think of the good things that were happening especially his relationship with Sarah which was getting more and more serious as time went by. He was also pleased, for the most part, with the business mainly because of the response to the ProForma. He needed to think of another marketing idea as it appears the beer plan was working out. Referrals worked well for him when he was a broker with Merrill. Perhaps he could come up with a plan that centers around referrals.

He went through his usual morning ritual and took of to work. When he saw Sarah he thought about how wonderful the evening would be having dinner with her. He hoped that she would be ok with ditching the secrecy about their relationship. Probably everyone knew about it anyway. Difficult thing to hide.

He was a bit worried that Judy might feel that he is spending more time with Sarah's needs than her needs. He decided to ask this morning. Judy replied that she was happy with the time and quality of the work he was doing for he and it was not a problem. John sighed a big sigh and that there was no problem.

John called Dayton to get the results of the business on Thursday. He was pleasantly surprised that he number was around $3000. Had he received the bank statement as yet and Dayton answered no. They wished each other a great weekend.

     PHILIP STEPHENS

There was a Hockey game on Saturday night in Windsor so he would invite Sarah to go with him. He wanted to find if she loved Hockey as much as he did. Under better circumstances he would have invited Dayton and Maude to go with them. He reminded himself that they had reached their goal of $100,000 in Limited Partnerships with the possibility of more to come.

After work was over at about 5pm he thought about stopping at the florists and buying a dozen red roses to give to Sarah when he picked her up. Neat thing to do. Chalk one up for the good guys.

CHAPTER FIFTY SIX

He got home at 6PM and checked the mailbox. Great! There was one envelope there and he opened it to find a check in the amount of $10,000 from one of his old clients. He thought about calling Dayton but he would see him tomorrow at the Pool Hall.

He took a quick shower and even shaved and used his best after shave. He left his apartment at 6:40 and arrived at Sarah's at 7 on the nose with his dozen red roses. When Sarah opened the door and accepted the roses She gave John a big hug and a really big kiss. What a wonderful surprise. I just love red roses.

Where to go for dinner was the question. They were both dressed to the nines so they decided to go to the most expensive restaurant in Windsor, "Ontarios"it was known for its prime beefsteak. They ordered Vodka Gibson's and they had two of them. Both ordered steaks medium rare with a baked potato. They really enjoyed their dinner and ordered a Grand Marnier after dinner drink. They left Ontario at 8Pm and headed back to Sarah's apartment. They couldn't wait to get in the door to undress for the best sex of their lives.

After a good deal of rest after sex John brought up the subject of addressing the matter of making public their relationship. Sarah said no need to do that. Everyone knows. Big surprise to John but he was glad. They only been dating for a few months but the outcome was clear to both of them; marriage! Who was going to bring it up? It would be John but not until he buys the ring next week. How exciting for both of them.

He asked Sarah if she would go to the Hockey game tomorrow night which began at 7:30. They would eat at a small Italian restaurant that Sarah really likes at 5:30. Have a half bottle of wine and maybe pizza or pasta. He would pick her up at 5PM if that was all ok with her. Of course, she answered in the affirmative. They hugged and kissed and said good night and Sarah thanked John for the roses.

When John got home he was too excited to go to sleep so he poured a small amount of Scotch and sipped it before going to bed with a huge smile on his face.

CHAPTER FIFTY SEVEN

Why wait till next week to buy the ring? He would purchase it today and give it to her after the Hockey game. He looked on line for jewelry stores in Windsor and picked the one with the largest ad for engagement rings and called them to get directions. He had no idea what to buy or how much to spend. He just thought he would know it when he saw it. He had two cups of coffee and drove to the jewelry shop. It was an elegant looking edifice which gave him confidence he was at the right place. He told the man behind the counter that he wanted to buy an engagement ring but he had no idea what kind so he said he was open to suggestions.

He brought out six different rings which he said were from one karat to two karats and the cost was between $2000 to $5000. Of course John picked the biggest one in the group and the cost was $5000. No problem for John. He paid for it with his credit card showing the man his new drivers license as proof.

John was beside himself with what he had just purchased and couldn't wait to give it to Sarah. He made his way to the Pool Hall. When he got there he immediately went to the office to look at the ledger book. Dayton was there and he asked about the Bank statement. Dayton went to the desk and opened one of the drawers and pulled out the Bank Statement. John spent a good deal of time comparing the entries in the ledger book to the entries on the Bank statement and they all matched

　　　PHILIP STEPHENS

which was a relief. John had mailed all the Limited Partner checks to the Bank and they all appeared. It was great to see the large balance. The take for Friday was around $3200 which was more in line with the number that Plummer said it was on weekends. John was relieved that he didn't have to question Dayton about the short fall in revenue. He did tell Dayton about the results of the questionnaire which Dayton said was encouraging. The Bank statement showed all of the deposits except for the $10,000 he had just received. Dayton seemed very pleased with the total of $115,000. John noticed the salary payments in the ledger and they seemed ok also. The Partnership check book remains in the office.

Maybe it was getting close to the time to seek another acquisition. John was thinking waiting another few days before he asked Dayton to explore the options for the purchase of a bar. They hugged each other and said they would keep in touch.

CHAPTER FIFTY EIGHT

On the way home John stopped and bought today's newspaper. He wanted to catch up with the goings on in Windsor. He spent about 45 minutes reading the paper and didn't see anything out of the ordinary. The fact that Fall was approaching was noted in the paper. It was now late in the afternoon and he decided to get ready to leave to pick up Sarah to eat dinner at the Italian restaurant. He had decided to give the ring to Sarah when they got home from the game. He would leave at 4:30.

Sarah was ready at 5 so they drove to the restaurant. It was a quaint looking restaurant and looked like a good choice thought John. They ordered two glasses of Italian wine and waited a bit before ordering. They decided not to order pizza. They ordered pasta dishes, a house salad and garlic bread. They ate slowly and ordered another round of garlic bread and two more glasses of wine. John was pleasantly surprised at how good the food was and told Sarah that her choice of restaurants was a good one.

It was now 6:45so they left the restaurant and made their way to the Hockey arena. It was crowded but they managed to get pretty good seats. The game was a close one which John enjoyed. He asked Sarah if she was enjoying the game and she said she loved Ice Hockey and was enjoying the game. The game was over at 10PM so they made their way back to Sarah's apartment.

When they had settled in, Sarah made some decaf coffee and they sat on the couch. John, being old school, got down on one knee and gave her the box with the ring in it and asked Sarah to marry him. There were tears in Sarah's eyes when she said yes with great enthusiasm. They hugged and kissed and Sarah still had tears in her eyes.

John said he was not interested in a long engagement and thought a small wedding was the way to go. Sarah agreed with John and they spent some time talking about the wedding. John wanted to get married in the Episcopal Church he was attending. He would talk to the Rector tomorrow to set a date and confirm it with Sarah tomorrow. John had never met her parents and Sarah hoped they would go to her parents home in Windsor tomorrow so John could meet them.

They also talked about where they would live and John said it was time to purchase a home in the neighborhood they both liked. He would contact a real estate agent and they would go house hunting next Saturday and Sunday. What about a honeymoon and they both agreed that it would be a short one because of their work schedule and they would decide later where to go. Fall had arrived and that would be a perfect time for the honeymoon.

He would pick her up after Church and head for her parents house. Sarah said she would call them in the morning to give them a heads up. They were both very excited and talked a bit more about the wedding. It was getting late and they hugged and kissed and said good night.

CHAPTER FIFTY NINE

There was no mail in the mailbox when John returned home. It had been a magical evening and John was worn out so he went to sleep and set the alarm for 7AM. He slept like a baby and awoke at the sound of the alarm. He took a shower and brewed some coffee and was not hungry for anything else. He called Sarah and woke her up. He said he would be there at 10:30 to go to her parents home.

After Church he spoke to the Rector to set a date for the wedding. The best time for John was one month from the past Saturday so the Rector put it on the calendar. The Rector said he would like to meet Sarah one day this coming week so John made an appointment for Tuesday night at 6PM.

He arrived at Sarah's home at 10:20 and Sarah said she had called her parents and they were ok to come at about 11AM. John told her about the wedding date and it was perfect for Sarah. He also told her about meeting the Rector on Tuesday. Sarah held up her left hand to show John the ring and how happy she was about the coming wedding. She had already selected her maid of honor and, since the wedding would be small, she did not need bride's maids. Sarah asked if Dayton would be the Best Man and John said yes. He had not told Dayton of the engagement but would do so this afternoon.

They were on their way to Sarah's parents home and one could tell that John was nervous. Sarah's parents greeted them at the door with her

PHILIP STEPHENS

Father shaking John's hand and he Mom giving him a hug. Sarah's Mom had made some scones and they had hot tea and the scones. The mood was very light hearted and John and her parents seemed to be getting along quite well. Her parents had a bunch of questions to ask John and he was very forthcoming. Sarah told her parents about the wedding date and the Church where the wedding would be held. Her parents approved of the details. They visited some more and,after about 90 minutes, John and Sarah left to back to her apartment. They talked some more about a small party at the Church after the wedding.

They talked about the money situation and commingling of funds. Sarah was ok with that knowing that eventually John would have some good income from the Partnership. John would make the down payment for the purchase of the property. John needed to address the "elephant" in the room that is his imprisonment. So now was the time to do that. He asked Sarah to have a seat because John had something important to tell her. He shared that he had spent one year in jail for giving Dayton some of his pain pills to help Dayton be able to play hockey with a broken foot. He never believed that he was doing anything illegal. The authorities indicted John for distribution of a controlled substance. He was paroled after spending one year in a minimum style prison. It caused his wife to divorce him and he his visiting rights to see his children. Dayton was suspended for 4 months from playing hockey. It has been a difficult for John and his parents and his brother who lives in Florida. His Parents continue to live in Brooklyn. He wished he could put all this behind him but that was not possible. He has to stay in touch with his parole officer periodically but he is able to work in Canada but not as a Consultant. John went on to say that he hopes this does not affect their marriage.

Sarah, of course, was taken back big time what John had to say. She needed some time to digest John's story and she asked John if he would leave while she processes the story.

So John leaves with his "tail between his legs" hoping for the best outcome.

PHILIP STEPHENS

CHAPTER SIXTY

Monday arrives with no word from Sarah. They were cordial to each other but he notices she is not wearing his ring when they meet. Later on in the morning, she tells John that they need to talk after work today so they agree to meet at a neighborhood watering hole after work. John is worried big time but there is not much he can do about the situation. The day drags by and eventually 5 PM comes and they both leave the office to meet at the appointed place,

Sarah does all the talking. She begins by saying that she was completely blind sided by John's story. She can empathize with John in regard to his not believing that he had done anything wrong but the law is the law and there is no getting away from that. She told her parents and they were shocked but did in some way understand the circumstances under which he served one year in jail. They felt that John has been given a second chance and he is apparently taking advantage of that so the bottom line is that Sarah has to make a choice of sticking with the wedding plans knowing the story.

Sarah continues to say that she truly loves John and that the one misstep should be disregarded in her decision to go ahead with their plans. John had tears in his eyes and tried to control his emotions but was unable. He said that he was so happy with her decision that he had no words to express his emotions. They hugged and John noticed that she had the engagement ring on her finger and would wear it to work tomorrow. Sarah said one more thing John had to do was to tell the Office Manager the full story and hoped it would not make a difference. So they parted ways and said see you tomorrow.

When Sarah and John got to work everyone noticed the engagement ring and offered their congratulations to both of them. John walked into the Manager's office and told him the whole story. The manager was taken back by that revelation and said it would be ok with him but he needed to tell his superiors and would get back to him.

John was on ":pins and needles" all day long. At the end of the day the Manager called John into his office and told him that The Bank said that since the event did not happen in Canada and, even if it did, Canadian law would not have prosecuted him. John could keep his job. He thanked him and went to tell Sarah that all was ok. See you tomorrow.

John left the office and headed for the Pool Hall to tell Dayton about the engagement and the wedding plans. He asked Dayton to be his Best Man and Dayton agreed. John took a deep breath and realized he had dodged a bullet.

CHAPTER SIXTY ONE

First thing in the morning he asked his Manager to recommend a good mortgage banker which he did and called them immediately. He wanted to be pre-approved on a mortgage. The Bank said they could take the information over the phone which he gave them. He said he had $55,000 in cash, had a monthly income of $1800 per month plus he was one of two General Partners that owned a Pool Hall valued at $115,000 plus a cash balance of $160,000. He gave them the name of his banker. You need to call my intended wife to get her financials. He told Sarah to expect a call from the Mortgage Bank regarding her financials. John had no idea of how much Sarah earned and what her net worth was.

Nothing unusual happened the rest of the day. At 4Pm John got a call from The Mortgage Bank saying that with a 10% down payment they could afford a home purchase at $300,000. He would call Sarah and give her the news He could afford a down payment of $20,000. Could she make up the difference? Maybe there is middle ground. He called her after he got home and gave her the information. She said she could afford $10,000. John said if needed he could come up with another $5000. They were prepared to go house hunting on the weekend, It was all very exciting. John went to the mailbox and found another envelop with a check for $5000. Making the total $120,000. If he found himself strapped for cash, he and Dayton could take a payment from the Partnership account.

John told Dayton that they needed another marketing tool to push things along and also think about buying a bar. What were their options on purchasing a bar? Dayton said he had two options, one at $70,000 and one at $75,000 and they could look at them any time they needed to. John was thinking next Sunday late in the morning like 11AM. Would that work for Dayton? He said yes and they would meet at 11AM at the Pool Hall.

John hoped that there might be more Limited Partnership money coming in. Perhaps both John and Dayton needed to come up with an additional list. He also thought about paying the Limited Partners a finders fee if they referred someone to us who purchases a Partnership. The fee would be 15%. If Dayton agreed John would type up a finders fee agreement which would be printed and sent out. Dayton said what a great idea. He would come by at 5:30 to pick up more stationary and envelopes to use for the finders fee plan.

When he saw Dayton he told him about the additional $5000 commitment. He asked Dayton how things were going with the beer promotion today and Dayton said thought very well. He looked at the ledger book and there were no surprises. He took the stationary and the envelopes with him.

CHAPTER SIXTY TWO

No letters in the mailbox, He began to develop the finders fee letter and it didn't take too long to go print 20 copies of which 17 were needed now. He had their addresses so he put the letters in the envelopes and sealed them He had the necessary stamps.

When he got to work he mailed them at the post office which was next door. Being Thursday he needed to make weekend plans with Sarah other than going house hunting. Sarah said she would cook dinner on Saturday night and they could go out to eat on Sunday. John still felt a bit of tension even though Sarah had agreed to continue wedding plans. No wonder after all John's story could have been a deal breaker.

The take from the pool hall continued to be in the neighborhood of what it was historically perhaps a bit higher. Both John and Dayton were well pleased with the totals which was about $22000.average per week. Maybe there could be a referral plan using the current patrons to bring new customers to the Pool Hall. John would think about it.

When he got home he called his parents, his brother Pete and Paul to give them the news about the wedding which was going to be a rather intimate affair. They will get a wedding invitation but not expected to attend. Wedding gifts would be allowed with money as the best gifts no matter how small. They will be house hunting this weekend as they both live in apartments. Some where along the way John would send pictures of the bride and groom. They were planning a brief honeymoon somewhere in the mountains in Quebec. This is a wonderful time to visit Quebec because it is in the fall and not too cold.

The calls took about an hour and a half to complete and it would be around 7PM. John had a sandwich and a bowl of soup for supper. He would watch the Maple Leafs versus the Canadians on TV and then go to sleep.

CHAPTER SIXTY THREE

Friday is here and John would be busy. He needed to talk to Sarah about their plans for Friday night and the weekend… John had found a wonderful Hotel in the Laurentides mountains in Quebec. He would call them today and make a reservation for a week beginning October 11th. A call to Dayton provided John with the latest figures on receipts from the Pool Hall. The numbers were encouraging. He was hopeful that the finders fee promotion would bear some big fruit. The numbers for the week were a total of $21,000.

He told the manager that the wedding is scheduled for October 10th and they would be out on a honeymoon the following week beginning October 11th. John thought it could be cold in Quebec in early October so they needed to bring winter clothing just in case. John needed to buy a mackinaw and boots. He would ask Sarah what she needed to buy as the weather might be on the cool side, There could be snow on the ground so skiing could be a possibility. Sarah, who has lived in Canada her whole life, no doubt could ski but John has never skied. There was only two weeks left before the wedding so they need to get all the bases touched.

John did not bring lunch today so he invited Sarah to have lunch with him to go over details of the wedding and to plan the weekend. Over lunch John reminded Sarah to make sure the invitations had been sent out and her parents had hired a caterer for the after wedding reception. Sarah had told John a few days ago that she had a good friend who was a real estate sales person who would be with them this coming weekend exploring the market. She said her friend Julie would pick them up at 9AM on Saturday at Sarah's apartment. John was so excited that they were going to buy a home especially if they could find one in their chosen neighborhood. John did not sense any actions from Sarah which might cause her second thoughts. Sarah had offered to cook dinner, for the first time for John, so she asked John to be there at 6:30PM.

After lunch John called Dayton just to check in. He told him that they were going house hunting on the weekend and he didn't know if he would have time to be at the Pool Hall on the weekend. Dayton said no problems at the Hall and the revenue was holding steady. John said that there were no subscriptions for Limited Partnerships the past few days. Judy asked John if he could type a few letters for her before he went home and he answered that he would be happy to, Usually on Friday there were not a lot of calls coming in for the ladies and today was no exception.

CHAPTER SIXTY FOUR

ohn left the office at 5:15 after finishing the letters for Judy. When he got home he checked the mail box and found one letter with a check in there for $5000 and it was from a referral which overjoyed John as the total was now $125,000. He was looking forward to Sarah's cooking as he knew she would be great. He purchased a bottle of wine on the way to Sarah's. It was her favorite red wine a Merlot.

Sarah seemed to be in a great mood when John arrived and she accepted the wine with a thank you asking John to open it to let it breath for a while. The smell from the kitchen was wonderful and John expected Sarah to hit a home run. He was patiently waiting for Sarah to say dinner was ready. It didn't take long as Sarah said to bring the wine to the table.

The meal started with a scrumptious Caesar salad. The main course was chicken marsala which he thoroughly was enjoying. She also made some garlic bread a favorite of his. The wine was also a big hit as they almost consumed the whole bottle.

John spent some time going over the wedding plans again just to be sure everything was taken care of. He asked if her parents had ordered flowers for the wedding and she said they had. He talked a bit about the hotel in Quebec they would be staying in and the possibility of cold weather and perhaps even snow. She needed to bring a winter coat and boots. They would be driving there so there would be no problem with luggage. They could bring whatever they wanted as there would be plenty of room. John was very effusive in his comments about how wonderful the meal was but what about dessert? Sarah had gone to the neighborhood bakery and purchased a cheese cake for desert which John loved.

John helped with the dishes and they sat in the living room with a cup of coffee. Again he was blown away by the meal he just ate and made it clear to Sarah that everything was perfect. After coffee they embraced and kissed a lot leading to sex which they had not had in several days. John was especially amorous and Sarah was the same. All John could think of was thank God they were both very happy.

They said their goodnights and John said he would see her tomorrow at 9AM.

CHAPTER SIXTY FIVE

John checked the mailbox and it was empty. He was still celebrating Sarah's culinary skills and what he could look forward to after they were married. A little over a week to go. He was tired and full and, knowing that tomorrow and Sunday would be busy days, he went to bed a bit early. Tomorrow came in a hurry as his alarm rang at 7:30. He showered and shaved and, after surveying his hair, he decided he needed to get a haircut next week. He would ask his Manager where to get a haircut.

He was really looking forward to the house hunting event hoping that Sarah's friend had picked out some nice homes at about $300,000 as that is all they could afford. On the way to Sarah's he stopped and picked up Sunday's paper which is always ready on Saturday. It would not be up to date on sports and news but that was ok. He wanted to see the Real Estate section before going out on Sunday.

John tried to remember what he wanted his home to look like but he drew a blank except it needed at least two bedrooms and a den to be used as an office for both he and Sarah. He did want it to be on one level he thought. He thought he should have asked Sarah what she wanted so, between the two of them, they could tell the Real Estate lady what the wanted to see.

John knocked on Sarah's door and she let him in embracing him and a soft kiss. The Agent had not yet arrived so he asked Sarah what she was looking for in a home. She said when I see it I will know that it is what I want. What a great idea! John should think that way also. The door bell rang and it was the Real Estate Agent he presumed. Sarah introduced John and Julie and they all took a seat. Julie asked them what they were looking for and John said that it could not cost more their mortgage was approved for and that was $300,000 preferably one story.

Julie said I have a number of homes to show you which meet your criteria so lets get going. They made several stops and so far neither John nor Sarah were impressed. The next house they visited was priced at $295,000 and was one story with two bedrooms and an office space. It was exactly what John had envisioned. Sarah also thought it had possibilities. It was now after 1PM and they were all tired so Julie took the handout of the house and said she has a few more houses to show them tomorrow. John said he could be available at 10:30 tomorrow so Julie said she would be there at Sarah's at 10:30. She then drove them back to Sarah's apartment and left them there.

John and Sarah both said that they really liked the last house they saw and it would be their pick if nothing they saw tomorrow was better. John said we have not had lunch yet and it was 2pm so they decided to grab an early dinner at the deli and then go home to their respective apartments and be ready to go again tomorrow morning.

CHAPTER SIXTY SIX

John was tired when he got home. He checked the mailbox and it was empty. He changed clothing and took some time to think about the last house they saw. It had everything that John wanted and Sarah liked it also so let's see what tomorrow brings. He lay down on the couch and turned on the TV and watched an old movie that would be over at 8:30 and then he could read the Real Estate adds in the paper he had bought that morning. Nothing seemed to interest him so he thought time to go to bed early. Well he had a hard time falling asleep but finally he did.

He had set the alarm for 7:30 on Sunday and he awoke at 7 so he turned the alarm off. He showered and shaved and had a cup of coffee before he got dressed for Church. He got to Church early and ran into the Rector who reminded him that the wedding was in a few days on October 10th. John said he couldn't wait. He was so excited. He asked the Priest how much of a donation he should give to the Church and the Rector said whatever you feel is appropriate.

Church was over at 10:05 so he drove to Sarah's and got there a bit early. He rang the bell and Sarah answered and she just looked gorgeous. John hugged her big time and said how lucky they are to find a house that they both liked. Sarah said maybe they will find a better one today. Julie arrived promptly at 10:30 and off they went to look at what Julie had picked for them. The first house they saw was similar to the house they saw last on Saturday but it was $305,000 but they would consider it. They saw three more houses which neither of them liked so the house they saw earlier today and the last one they saw yesterday were the ones to pick from. John and Sarah both said the one they would choose is the one they say yesterday and told Julie. She said that she would call the seller's agent and offer $290,000. She got on her phone and made the call. The other agent said that she would call back in less than an hour so they headed back to Sarah's apartment to await the call. They barely made it back there when Julie's phone rang, she answered it and listened for a few seconds and hung up. She turned to them and said you just bought yourselves a home for $290,000.

Julie knew that they were to be married next Saturday so she had to get the house inspected before they left on their honeymoon. The closing would happen once they were back in Windsor. They thanked Julie and she said she would call once the inspection was completed.

Julie left and John and Sarah celebrated by jumping up and down and screaming whatever. It was only 2PM so they decided to have a "little roll in the hay" before going to dinner to really celebrate. The sex was wonderful for both of them and they showered together got dressed and went to dinner. After a magnificent meal at The French Connection they went back to Sarah's and said good night and John went home for a good nights sleep.

CHAPTER SIXTY SEVEN

The morning came quickly for John as the alarm rang at 6:45. He lay awake thinking of the events of yesterday. He thought how lucky he was to be in Ontario, having a beautiful girl friend, a great job and a wonderful business. Thank God for all the blessings in his life.

It was less than a week till the wedding and he was getting a bit nervous which was to be expected. He needed to start getting his gear ready for the honeymoon and he would start tonight. Was there anything he needed to buy? He would think about that during the day. He showered and shaved and had two cups of coffee while he was dressing to go to work.

He got to work at 8:05 and he saw that Judy and Sarah were already there. Sarah was on the phone so John would wait til she got off the phone to say hello and give her a kiss. He called Dayton to see how things were going. Dayton said they were really busy over the weekend and the revenue was over $8,000. John said he would stop by today after work to talk about his honeymoon and the purchase of a bar. Did Dayton zero in on the choices? Dayton replied they could talk about it this evening. Sarah was off the phone so John greeted her in the usual way. Was she excited about the coming wedding? John asked her if she was nervous about the wedding and the honeymoon and she answered of course she was.

During the day some of the guys asked him if he was nervous and they all got the same answer. Of course. He was certain that Sarah received the same question. Sarah,too, was also thinking if there was something else to buy for the honeymoon She could not think of anything but she would consider that question.

They kept very busy as the phones were active because the market was up big time and people were calling asking why was the market up so big. The answer was the US GDP was better than expected. He barely had time to go to lunch. Sarah stayed busy most days and rarely ate lunch unless she brought a sandwich. When 5PM came John told Sarah that he was going to the Pool Hall and would call her later.

John told Dayton that he had not gotten more referral letters but it was early. He reminded Dayton at what time he needed to be at the Church on Saturday. John had the rings and would give them to him on Saturday. He also gave Dayton the information regarding the Hotel they would be at on their honeymoon in case he needed to call him. They would be back in town on the 17th. They would be staying at a local hotel the night of the wedding and drive to the Hotel in Quebec on Sunday.

Dayton talked about the bars he had scoped out. They could visit them when he returns to Windsor which was ok with John. John hoped when he returns there would be a few letters in his mailbox.

     PHILIP STEPHENS

CHAPTER SIXTY EIGHT

ohn checked the mailbox and found two letters both for $5000 one from the original lists and one was a referral bringing the total to $135,000. Wow what a number! John decided to call the Hotel to check on what the weather would be on the honeymoon. They told him no snow and the temperature would be a high in the upper 50's and a low in the lower 50's. John called Sarah and gave her the news about the weather. She had better bring a heavy sweater in addition to a mackinaw. Probably a wool hat also.

Since they both have a lot of preparation to do this week, they probably shouldn't be eating dinner together. They should plan to have lunch together most days to talk about the trip and any questions or concerns. He wanted to keep Sarah appraised of the goings on with the Partnership especially about the Limited Partnerships which was now at $135,000. Also he told her that Dayton had found three possible bars they would look at when they return. Did she have any questions at this time and she answered not at this time. She was getting more and more excited every minute and so was he, See you tomorrow said John.

John started to get together the clothes, etc that he would bring on the honeymoon. He found a place in his apartment where he could stow all the stuff. He would wait until Thursday or Friday to put his toiletries where the clothes were, So far he has not needed to buy anything else for the trip.

He did call Dayton to tell him about the two more Partners he received making the total $135,000. How was the beer promotion doing today? Dayton said very well as usual. Was there anything he could do to help John with the wedding and the trip said Dayton. John said not so far. Dayton also remarked how well the Limited Partnerships were proceeding well above their goal. Counting the two new Partnerships the cash balance in their account is about $220,000 which is great.

Dayton told John that they needed to find someone to be the Manager of the bar they would purchase. Perhaps one of the bartenders at that bar could be the Manager? We will see what options there are but first we have to purchase a bar or maybe two. We have to consider that our cash flow right now is about $22,000 per week and that will increase when we make our next purchase or purchases.

CHAPTER SIXTY NINE

t lunch today John and Sarah needed to talk about the wedding and the honeymoon. John had called the Rector to ask if there was a need for wedding rehearsal and the Rector said that, since it was a small affair with just the bride and groom and the best man and maid of honor, it was not necessary. The Rector said to be there at the Church one half hour ahead of time. John gave that information to Sarah since she would be going with her parents and he would be coming alone. He needed to remind Dayton as to what time to be there on Saturday. They talked a bit about the furnishings etc they would have to buy for their new home and said they could talk about on there way to the Hotel in Quebec. Since this was a small wedding with only seven people there the caterer was not needed so Sarah said she would tell her Mom and Dad. Even if a few more folks showed up an after wedding caterer would not be needed.

When John returned from lunch he called Dayton to tell him to be at the Church at 9:30 on Saturday. Dayton said he and Maude would be there at 9:30. Dayton assured John that everything would be ok while he was on his honeymoon. The Manager called John into his office to ask if it would be ok if he and his wife came to the wedding. John said of course they would be welcome. He gave him the name of the Church and the time of the ceremony. John reminded the Manager that they would be back at work the 19th of October. Sarah said that Judy wanted to come to the wedding and she told her that would be great.

The afternoon was uneventful and Sarah and John kissed and said see you tomorrow. John stopped at the drug store on the way home to pick up a few things for the trip. He bought a package of condoms to be sure he had enough for the trip. He didn't think a pregnancy would be happening just yet.

There was no mail in the mailbox. John didn't have anything to eat in the fridge so he turned around and headed for the diner where he had a nice dinner. He returned home, after buying a newspaper where he saw the Maple Leafs were playing so he turned on the TV at 7:30 and watched the game which ended at 10PM.

CHAPTER SEVENTY

The rest of the week went by without any problems or concerns. It was Friday in the morning and John was satisfied that he had gotten together all that he needed for the honeymoon. He thought that perhaps he and Sarah needed to get together Friday for a quick dinner at the Deli so he asked her and she accepted. They drove there in separate cars and got there at about the same time.

John said to Sarah that this was her last chance to back out of the wedding and she said, with emphasis, no way Jose. They kidded around for a while and ate their dinner. There was little to be said at that point and they kissed and hugged and said goodnight and pleasant dreams on the last night they would be sleeping alone the whole night and for days and months and years.

Don't think that either one had a good nights sleep as they were too excited and a bit apprehensive about what would take place tomorrow morning. Both John and Sarah would take their wedding attire with them to Quebec with the thought they could wear those clothes at least once on their honeymoon.

Both awoke early on Saturday with great anticipation of the coming wedding. Each tried to push the clock ahead but not possible. The time would arrive in its own sweet time. John had packed a bit before retiring and finished that morning. He kept thinking that he must have forgotten some things. Surely Sarah was thinking the same thing.

They both arrived at the same time and hugged each other. Sarah's parents were very solicitous of John saying that their daughter and he made for the perfect couple. John thanked them and assured them that they would be very happy.

The tine came for the ceremony to begin. Everyone took their places as pointed out by the Rector. Dayton gave John the rings when it was appropriate and the bride and the groom placed the rings on each other fingers. The Rector pronounced them Man and Wife. They kissed each other passionately and everyone clapped and cheered.

The attendees lingered for a while until John said they thanked everyone for attending and they were off to their Hotel to spend the night before leaving to go on their honeymoon. And so another chapter in John's and Sarah's life would begin.

CHAPTER SEVENTY ONE

Once they got into John's car, they kissed and kissed for what seemed like an eternity. John made their way to the Hotel where the bellmen helped bring their luggage to their room. John said they needed to go to bed early because they would get up at the crack of dawn to drive a long way to Quebec. They did got to bed early but not to sleep but to "consummate" their marriage. They were very sweet to each other after sex and they fell asleep in each others arms.

The awoke at 6AM, showered and John shaved. They decided to eat a big breakfast so they didn't need to worry about lunch. They dressed casually and closed their suitcases and called for the bellmen to take their luggage to their car. They left the Hotel at 8AM on to another adventure in their lives. John had gotten directions from the Hotel in Quebec but he used the map app on his cell phone as a backup. John had some CD's that he brought with him to listen to music on the drive, It would be a long drive stopping only for gas and a potty break.

The weather was good with a clear sky and the temperature was in the low 60's. They had decided to talk about and to make a list of the furniture and appliances they would need in their new home. Sarah had pen and paper ready. They began to make that list but they knew they would not account for every thing. Biggest item was the King size bed. They could use all the furniture from Sarah's apartment but John's stuff was part of the lease. They also was not sure what the current home owners would take with them especially the washer and dryer. They had Sarah's TV but they needed one for the bedroom. When they got back home they would need to check on the closing date. They would not move out until the end of the month so long as the closing date was near the end of the month.

They stopped a number of times to stretch their legs and buy gas and a potty break. The time flew by and the weather cooperated. When they arrived at the Hotel, the weather was a bit cooler than in Windsor. It was a huge Hotel with lots of flowers and trees. They checked in and the bellmen brought all their luggage to their room which was the honeymoon suite. It was magnificent. They surveyed the room and were very pleased. After resting for about an hour, they went down to the dining room for dinner.

They loved the choices on the menu, ordered wine and relaxed before ordering dinner. They made excellent choices and enjoyed the dinner. After dinner they went to the bar and had an after dinner drink. They were real tired and they went to their room and went to bed in each others arms.

CHAPTER SEVENTY TWO

Early the next morning John got a phone call from Paul.

He first congratulated John and Sarah on their marriage. He said the main reason he was calling was because he got to thinking about John's last call regarding the trust worthiness of Dayton. So he decided to write an amendment to the Partnership which said that neither of the General Partners could take any money out of the Partnership to their benefit without both signatures of the General Partners. He would send one copy to Dayton and send one copy to you by FedEx to your Hotel in Quebec and send it back to me by FedEx asap. I will ask Dayton to do the same. If Dayton wonders why this is necessary, I will tell him that it is in both parties interest to do this. He was acting as attorney to the Partnership.

John said he thought that in a Partnership it would not be legal for one General Partner to do that. Paul said that he was just being cautious in the matter and not to be concerned. Look for it tomorrow and send it back right away by FedEx. John said he would do that. Paul said he would notify their Banker in Windsor about the amendment.

John told Sarah about the call and she was concerned about that issue. Do you think Dayton would do that said Sarah as she was not very trusting of Dayton. John said it was a good idea to be careful. He would look for the overnight package tomorrow.

It looked like a pretty day with the sun shining and not a cloud in the sky. In the lobby they had a board with the current temperature on it. It read 52 degrees which is ok. They went into the dining room to eat breakfast. It was served buffet style with lots of fruit, scrambled eggs, bacon, sausage, pancakes and a waffle maker. John was in heaven as he loves breakfast food and ate every thing on the buffet. Sarah just ate some scrambled eggs and some bacon. They both had orange juice and coffee.

After breakfast they decided to walk the grounds but they needed to put on heavy sweaters. The grounds were beautiful with lots of flowers, bushes and all kinds of trees. There was a bridge going over a stream and they walked over that to what looked like a Japanese garden. It was truly a gorgeous scene. They went back to the lobby and asked were there any special activities today. They said there was a hayride at 4PM with blankets and hot cocoa. There was a movie in the auditorium at 1PM and a buffet lunch at noon. Lots to do and lots to eat. They decided to do all the above. After the hayride they went back to the room where they rested for a while and then had amazing sex. They showered and headed for the dining room to eat dinner.

CHAPTER SEVENTY THREE

There was a rib eye steak on the menu so they both ate that for dinner along with a Caesar salad and a baked potato. They had shrimp cocktail as an appetizer. The dessert was a choice of chocolate cake or crème brule. They had decaf coffee also.

After dinner they had a dance band in the entertainment area. John and Sarah had never danced together so they gave it a whirl. They had so much fun dancing they stayed there for an hour. They were big time tired when the left the dance floor to go for an after dinner drink in the bar.

While in the bar, they talked about the amendment to the Partnership. They wondered what Dayton was thinking and if he would sign it. Sarah brought the trust factor again but John was still trusting Dayton until he had reason to think otherwise. He would call Paul in a few days to see if Dayton had signed the amendment. He thought he would also call Dayton tomorrow to check on him and the revenue for the Pool Hall.

They were really enjoying their honeymoon. It was time to hit the sack so they went to their suite and did, in fact, go to sleep looking forward to another fun filled day and the package.

When morning came, John got dressed and told Sarah he was going down to the lobby to check on the events of the day. He found out that there was a bus trip that would tour the countryside that would leave at 10Am. Lunch would be provided. One had to sign up at the desk which he did. He picked up a newspaper waiting for Sarah to come down for breakfast. Nothing exciting in the paper except the stock market in the US was still doing well.

Sarah arrived in about twenty minutes and they made their way to the dinning room. John told her about the bus trip at 10AM and she thought it would be fun. In the dinning room there was a guy making omelets which they both ordered after standing on line for about ten minutes. They also helped themselves to some fruit and bacon and sausage. It was a super breakfast, They went to their room to change for the bus trip.

The bus left the Hotel pretty full. There was a guide at the front of the bus telling them what they would see today. The scenery along the way was beautiful. The first stop was to be at some caves deep in the mountains. They left the bus and walked into the cave. It was pretty cold in there and were amazed at the size of the cave. The further they walked into the cave the colder it got but they were comfortable with their heavy sweaters on.

       PHILIP STEPHENS

CHAPTER SEVENTY FOUR

John was hoping that when they got back to the Hotel this afternoon the FedEx package would be there. In the meantime there were enjoying the many sites along the way. The Hotel had supplied lunch boxes for the passengers so they stopped at a picnic area to eat lunch. There was also bottles of water supplied. The lunch hit the spot and, after about an hour, the bus continued along the way. One stop was at waterfall which was magnificent and then to beautiful garden that had all vanities of flowers, shrubs and trees. They got to leave the bus and walk around. It reminded John of the gardens in Dallas like the Arboretum. The guide told them they would now make their way back to the Hotel.

I took about an hour to get to the Hotel and it was now 3PM, John went to the desk to look for the FedEx package and it was there. He opened it up, read the amendment and signed it. He had it notarized and gave it to the desk to have it sent to Paul by FedEx. They went to their room to rest before going to dinner. John called Paul on his cell to tell him he had sent the package back to him. Had he heard from Dayton? Paul answered no but it was too soon to get the amendment from him.

The food at the Hotel was top drawer and there was lobster on the dinner menu. They both loved lobster so they ordered it along with some wine and Caesar salad. The lobster was better than expected. They decided to skip dessert. The band was there again so they danced for a bit of time and turned in. What a wonderful day. What would tomorrow bring? It had to be something great as the past few days was magical. The weather had been super with highs in the upper 50s. The sign in the lobby had promised good weather the rest of the week and,so far, that was true.

CHAPTER SEVENTY FIVE

I t was already Wednesday. The time was flying by and the old adage was true; "Time flies by when you are having fun". John would call Dayton today to check on things and to see if he has any remarks about the amendment, He called Dayton's number but there was no answer. He would try again later. There were tennis courts on the property so after breakfast they rented rackets, bought a can of balls and stepped onto one of the courts. Neither one of them were any good but it was fun just to play and get some exercise.

After playing tennis, they looked at the events of the day in the lobby. There was a movie at 4PM and bingo at 1Pm. They decided to do both. They went to their suite and showered and dressed and went off to breakfast. John was enjoying the breakfast buffet as much as anything they have experienced in the dining room. They took a walk around the grounds after finishing breakfast. Bingo was at 1PM and it was now 12PM. They decided to skip lunch as they had big breakfast. They were sure they were gaining weight.

Wonder if they have cash prizes at Bingo. They both enjoyed playing bingo but they play maybe once a year on vacation or at a Church. They played for about an hour and Sarah won a game and won $5; a big deal but it was fun. It was now 2:15 and the movie didn't start until 4PM. They took another walk around the property in a different direction. They stopped at a pond that had Koi and they just rested there until 3;45

and went to the movies. Thank goodness they had not seen the movie they were showing. The nice thing was they had popcorn available.

They enjoyed being quiet and watched the movie. After it was over they headed to the dining room as they were hungry as they did not eat lunch. The dinner was Italian style which they were most pleased with. John ordered lasagna while Sarah ordered chicken marsala; both excellent choices. They ordered a bottle of Chianti. It turned to be their favorite meal there.

They had a game room there so after dinner they went to that room and played gin rummy for about an hour. They went to their room and John was feeling amorous so they had, as usual, great sex and fell asleep at 10PM.

CHAPTER SEVENTY SIX

They slept in Thursday and had brunch in the dinning room at 10AM. John tried to call Dayton but no answer. What was going on? He was concerned because Dayton was always available. He did not have Maude's number so he called the Pool Hall. The bar tender answered and said Dayton has not been to work since Monday. Now John was really upset and didn't know what to do. Almost immediately after hanging up, his phone rang and it was Maude. She said Dayton was missing since Monday evening as he did not come home from work Monday evening, She called the police and reported him missing but they have not found him,

John was shocked and told Maude that they would cut their honeymoon short and be back in Windsor late Friday afternoon. John called Paul to see if he had received Dayton's amendment copy and he said no he had not. He told Paul that Dayton's wife called him to say that Dayton was missing since Monday and she notified the police. He said they were cutting their honeymoon short to be back in Windsor Friday afternoon. He would call when he had more information.

John told Sarah about Dayton and that they were returning to Windsor tomorrow and hoped that would be ok with her and she said of course. At least they had been at the Hotel since Sunday and had a great time but it was important that they got back to Windsor as soon as possible.

They just hung around Thursday with the weight of Dayton's disappearance on them. They managed to eat lunch and dinner and alerted the desk that they were having to check out early tomorrow morning and would they have a bill ready at that time.

They spent a good part of the afternoon packing up their stuff and didn't say very much to each other. It was a shame they had to leave a few days earlier than they had planned. Bummer.

CHAPTER SEVENTY SEVEN

They packed quickly wanting to get on the road as early as possible. They truly had a wonderful honeymoon but not looking forward what awaited them in Windsor. They wanted to have some breakfast before leaving. The porters helped load their car while John paid the bill. They said goodbye and off they went.

Perhaps Maude might call sometime today to give an update on the whereabouts of Dayton. Needless to say John was very concerned with all kinds of thoughts running through his mind. He was trying to be positive but that was difficult. Had Dayton taken all the money and leave the area? Did he sign the amendment? He called Paul and brought him up to date. Had he gotten the signed amendment from Dayton? The answer was no which didn't make John feel more positive. He would keep Paul in the loop and said goodbye.

They were making good time but he did not want to get a ticket which would slow them down. They stopped for gas almost immediately after leaving the Hotel. The weather was accommodating with no clouds only blue skies. They would have to make several stops for gas and potty breaks along the way but they should be in Windsor late in the afternoon.

It was about 10AM when the phone rang. It was Maude and she was hysterical. She was barely able to get the words out of her mouth. She said the police just called and said they had found Dayton's body in the marsh land. He had been shot in the head execution style and he was deceased. What a shock! John and Sarah could not believe what they had heard. What else did the police say asked John? Maude said they had no clues but were actively pursuing the case.

John told Maude that they would be back in Windsor late afternoon and would call when they got there, What to do? John had so many thoughts running around in his head. He called the Pool Hall and talked to the bartender. He gave him the news and said can he could manage until John got back to Windsor late in the day. Was he able to make deposits at the bank? He answered yes he did that.

No matter what the outcome of the investigation, John had to quit his job at Royal Bank as there was so much to attend to over the next few weeks. John asked Sarah to get out pen and paper and list the things John said needed attention. Before he got started, he called Paul and gave him the news. Paul said he would call him later in the day with the steps John had to take relative to the Partnership and said how sorry he was in Dayton's death.

John proceeded to make the list of things to do. The list was short at this time as John did not have the time to work the list. He knew he needed to hire another bartender and consider whether Tim could handle the running of the bar and could he recommend a bartender. Did Tim make the entrees in the ledger of the revenue of the past three days?

Get a letter to the Limited Partners about Dayton's death and everything was under control. He needed to bring the ledger up to date. Check the mail for bills that need to be paid was on the list. He needed to write the checks for one week of work for the employees. His head was swimming and out of control. He needed to get a grip and calm down. Sarah was most unhappy about John having to quit his job but she understood the reasons for doing that. She would try and be as helpful as possible.

John knew he had to contact the police after he finds out from Maude the name of the Detective who was leading the investigation. He would make an appointment to be in his office first thing in the morning. As far as today was concerned he needed to spend a good deal of time at the Pool Hall attending to a host of things.

Time moved quickly as John considered other things that needed attention. John told Sarah of what his plans were when they got to Windsor. They would go to see Maude and get whatever information she could give them including the name of the Detective. After that they would go to the Pool Hall and talk to Tim and check the other things on the list.

CHAPTER SEVENTY EIGHT

They arrived in Windsor at about 4:30 and went directly to see Maude. They gave big hugs to Maude and offered their condolences. Maude calmed down and shared the news again with them. The police said it was an execution and they had no clues or leads at this time but were anxious to talk to John. The name of the Detective was Jerald Brady and Maude gave John his phone number. John called Brady and set up an appointment for tomorrow at 9AM.

They continued their conversation with Maude. Did she know of someone who Dayton was having a problem with? She said that Dayton had money problems but did not know what that was about. Did she tell the Detective about that? She said yes. Was she making funeral arrangement for Dayton and she said she was getting help from Dayton's family. John said he would try to be of help to Maude but she needed to understand the pressure he was under regarding the partnership. They left Maude and headed for the Pool Hall. On the way he called his Banker and gave him the news. He was waiting to hear from his attorney the steps that need to be taken. He needed to tell Maude to get 6 copies of the death certificate when it is available.

They arrived at the Pool Hall at 6PM and John immediately talked to Tim. Would he consider, with a nice raise, to be the manager of the Pool Hall? Tim said it would depend on the money. John was behind the eight ball because he really needed Tim so he offered him a 40% raise which was acceptable to him. The next thing he did was to go over the ledger to be sure it was up to date. Tim had made the necessary entries regarding the revenue for the last few days. John checked Dayton's desk to check for any bills that needed to be paid. John would assume that job going forward coming to the Pool Hall a few times a week. John also checked to see in the 3 hole check book what his employees were paid and write out checks dated tomorrow for the employees.

Did Tim know of a bar tender they could hire to take the 2nd shift at the Pool Hall? In fact he was way ahead of him as he had contacted a good friend who would be a good hire. He would call him and have him come to the Pool Hall tomorrow at 1PM.

John thought if things worked out at the Hall, he might not have to quit his job. John asked Sarah to call the Real Estate person to check on the inspection and the closing date. They needed to visit both of their apartments to unload the luggage. They would stay at Sarah's apartment at least for tonight. The inspection went well and the closing date would be next Wednesday. He called the Mortgage guy to give him the news but he said he had already been contacted and the mortgage was approved.

On the way to John's apartment they stopped at the Deli for something to eat. The unloaded John's luggage and unpacked and got together a change of clothes for tomorrow and his dop kit. He checked the mail and there was two checks for $5000 each John would deposit at the Bank tomorrow. They left and proceeded to Sarah's place. They were dead tired but Sarah unpacked anyway and they went to sleep knowing tomorrow would be a very busy day.

CHAPTER SEVENTY NINE

They arose at 7:30 and John had to be at the Police Station at 9AM to see Detective Grady. The Detective asked about the relationship between himself and Mr. Hudson. He told him that they had known each for several years beginning in Dallas Texas. He was a client of mine and, when he moved to Windsor, we became partners in business. He knew very little about Dayton's private life but he did know his wife, Maude. He and Dayton had a very good relationship and trusted each other. Was there any problems in the Partnership? Asked Grady. John said not at first but recently he suspected Dayton of skimming the receipts from the Pool Hall they owned. He had no proof but Dayton knew he was being watched.

What made you think that he was not to be trusted asked Grady. John said that the take on a daily basis was about 20% lower than the original owner was taking in. John went on to say that Maude thought that Dayton was having money troubles. At the beginning of the Partnership they each put up $30,000. My end came from the sale of my home in Dallas plus the sale of several securities.

Do you think that he might have had a problem in coming up with the money asked the Detective. John said that Dayton was not making a lot of money as a hockey player for a minor league team in Dallas. He did not know of what assets he had to come up with the money.

John wanted to know if the information he was giving was helpful. Grady said very helpful. By the way where have you been this past week? I have been on my honeymoon in Quebec all week until yesterday. The Detective thanked him and asked for his phone number.

After the interview John went to his bank to deposit the two checks and to see his Banker. John wanted to know if the balance in the account was about $220,000. John told him about the murder of Dayton and that the Police were investigating it. No clues at this time. The Partnership will continue with only him as the General Partner. He would buy out his wife as the beneficiary of Dayton' share of the Partnership as she would not in any way benefit it. He was in consultation with his attorney regarding that matter. He would be using the same checks as before and the Manager of the Pool Hall would continue to make daily deposits. Here is my phone number in case you need to reach me.

CHAPTER EIGHTY

John needed to call Paul to check on the legal implications for the Partnership. He said he checked with an attorney in Ontario and found that Dayton's share of the Partnership would go into his Estate and his wife would no doubt be the beneficiary. If you do not want her to be your partner you will have to give her share. Both you and Dayton each put up $30,000. You will need to give her the $30,000 plus any income earned. What were the earnings of the Pool Hall during the time you owned it. John said about $44,000. So she is due half of that or $22,000 plus the $30,000 that Dayton put up. That is all she is entitled to. John said he would offer her the $42,000 today. She is not very sharp so she will take the money and run. However, they took out a loan of $60,000 which she is responsible for half of that being $30,000. So, the bottom line is that she is entitled to only $12,000. Am I correct. Paul said you are but you now have the responsibility for the $60,000 loan.

John checked in with Sarah telling her what had transpired and said he was on the way to the Pool Hall for the interview of the potential bar tender. He arrived at the Pool Hall a bit early so he wrote checks to the employees for the week. He told Tim that the new salary arrangement would be reflected on next week's check which Tim agreed with. John checked the ledger to be sure it was up to date. He also checked the mail to find a few bills that needed to be paid so he took out the checkbook

PHILIP STEPHENS

and wrote checks to cover the bills. He asked Tin to place mail in the in box on the desk and to keep the checkbook in the center drawer.

The interview with Roger Hall went well and he offered the job of first shift bar tender to him at the same salary that Tim had received prior to being appointed the Manager. Tim would give him the keys so he could open the Hall at 9AM. John was satisfied with the arrangement so he thought he ought consider not quitting his day job. Depending on the settlement with Maude, he would think about buying a bar.

He left the Pool Hall and made his way to see Maude. He told Maude about his conversation with Grady and she seemed pleased. Now about the settlement. You are responsible for one half of the loan that Dayton and I took on for the Partnership which is $30,000. You will have to pay the interest of that loan until it is paid off Dayton put in $30,000 plus the earnings in the Partnership over the time we have owned if is $52,000 of which your share is $26,000. Adding together the $30,000 plus the $22,000 it comes to $52,000 but you are responsible for the loan amount of $30,000 so the net to you is $22,000. That is the bottom line. I can write you a check for that amount and you will not be responsible for the loan of $30,000 I, as General Partner, will be responsible for the $60,000. She says I will let you know later today. Please call me.

CHAPTER EIGHTY ONE

I called Maude and she said she would decline the offer of $22,000. John was disappointed and said that she was being unreasonable. What would it take to remove you from the Partnership. She said $42,000. If you choose to stay in the Partnership, you will be responsible for the loan of $30,000. She said she knew that. Also you will not be able to take out money from the Partnership without my signature. I will counter your offer with my offer of $27,000. Take it or leave it. She accepted my offer. I told her that my attorney will draw up the document needed to complete this agreement. I will get back to you in a few days.

He called Paul and gave him the detail of the agreement giving her $27,000 which was meeting her demands half way. Would you please draw up the document and send it ASAP to the Pool Hall. I called Tim and asked him to call me when the FedEx package arrived. When I get the document, I will go to the Bank along with Maude to have the agreement notarized and to give her the check for $27,000.

I decided to sit down and do a cost analysis and revenue analysis for the Pool Hall:

Monthly revenue is about $75,000

Monthly expense are:

Salary is about $7500.

Liquor and beer is about $2000.

PHILIP STEPHENS

Heat and Air is about $2000'

Interest on loan is 200.

Referral fee is about $6000 which is a one time fee.

Total Expenses not including Referral fees is around $12,000

Net Profit before taxes is about $63,000 a month

Wow sure is a profitable business. The hit of $27,000 is also a one time charge.

He called Detective Brady to get an update on the case. He said that after interviewing several of Dayton's close friends, it appears that he was in trouble with money that he had borrowed. Brady needed to find out who loaned him the money and talked to that person as a person of interest.

John needed to give Sarah all the current news so he called her and said he was coming to her apartment now.

CHAPTER EIGHTY TWO

ohn went over the details of the agreement with Maude. Sarah said you probably did as well as you could and put it behind you. He also gave her the Balance sheet statement and she was really pleased. All the bases were covered at the Pool Hall so should he continue to work or quit and spend 100% of his time managing the Partnership working out of the office at the Pool Hall. She certainly had an opinion saying that he could manage both jobs right now and that may not be the case in the future.

Should he consider the purchase of the bar now or wait until there is more money in the account and the death of Dayton was somewhat in the rear window? He called Sarah to ask her that question and she agreed with him to wait for a month to consider that purchase.

Since today is Friday, the package from Paul will not be here until tomorrow so he would have to wait until Monday to get together with Maude. In the meantime he would draft a letter to the Limited Partners about Dayton's death and to assure everyone that things were under control.

He went back to the Pool Hall and check on the supply of stationary as he needed to send that letter. He thought he had enough but he called the printer to order another 100 sheets and envelopes. He needed to quit for the day and go home to his apartment to check the mailbox and then go to be with his wife.

There was no mail in the box so he went up to his apartment to get some more clothes to a take with him to Sarah's apartment. He couldn't wait to move into their new house. They should spend the weekend purchasing the items that were on their list that they knew they needed.

Sarah was already home when John got there. She said that she told the Manager that John would be back to work on Monday. She had a very busy day catching upon the events that occurred while they were away and to get in touch with some of her clients. John said he felt a bit more comfortable after some of his activities that day. He also shared what Brady had told him and it looked like he was on the right track with the investigation.

They went out to dinner and had a relaxing time at the restaurant. Amazing what a few glasses of wine could do to calm you down. They were looking forward to shopping tomorrow and purchasing items for their new home. They need to make arrangements with the moving company for next week's move.

CHAPTER EIGHTY THREE

I t was Saturday morning and they were going shopping in about an hour. He had some other things he needed to attend to.

At the end of the next month there would be a balance of over $256,000 in the account. So there needed to be a distribution to all of the Partners including himself. The $10,000 Limited Partners would each get $2500 and the $5000 Limited Partners would each get $1250 making a total distribution of $58000. The General Partner would get a distribution of $10000 the total being $68000 leaving a balance of over $188000 enough to purchase a bar. He needed to tell Sarah about the distribution in a month to all the Partners. She would get $2500 and I would get $10.000. Big time profits for the Partnership and an opportunity to purchase a bar. She was thrilled.

Before looking at purchasing a bar, John must retire the loan from the bank of $60,000. In doing this the balance is $128,000. After the $27000 given to Mrs. Hudson the balance would be $101000. The balance after the 2nd month will be $164000 enough to the bar.

John needed to find the list of bars that Dayton had scoped out. He would check that out at the Pool Hall after work tomorrow. He needed to call Brady again to see where the investigation is at this time. Brady said he has been interrogating a person of interest but no break in the case.

John went to the Pool Hall and look for the list of bars. He checked Dayton's desk and file cabinet but was unable to find the list. He asked Pete if he knew which bars Dayton was looking at. He said he had a pretty good idea who they were. Did he have any idea of what it would take to buy one? He said between $65000 and $75,000. Would he go with him next Saturday morning to look at the bars? Tim said ok but what time. John said I will meet you here at 9AM.

They got a bit of a late start to go shopping. They had a short list so they went to the local department store and bought a King size bed with a box frame. Apparently the owners were taking the washer and dryer so they needed to buy a washer and dryer. They went to Home Depot and bought the washer and dryer plus an outdoor grill. They went to a furniture store and bought a recliner plus a wing backed chair. They bough some kitchen ware and some other minor things.

It was now 1PM and they decided that was enough for the day. John needed to check things out at the Pool Hall so they made a stop there only spending an hour there. They were hungry so they stopped for lunch at the Deli and had a super lunch. They went back to Sarah's and talked a little more about stuff they needed for the house. They decided to wait until all the furniture from Sarah's apartment had been moved before deciding what else they needed. They were looking forward to taking possession next week.

CHAPTER EIGHTY FOUR

While they were chilling John's phone rang and it was Detective Brady. He said they had made an arrest on the killing of Dayton. It seems that Dayton owned him a bunch of money and had stopped paying him so Dayton was killed for that reason. John was pleased to hear the news and hoped the man, whoever he was, would be found guilty if the case went to trial. Maybe the guy signed a confession so the trial; would be about sentencing. He told Sarah and she was happy also.

Next week came and the home deal was closed and they took possession of their home. They were overjoyed. Sarah made arrangements to have all of her stuff packed and delivered to the new home. John called the stores where they had purchased stuff and asked them to deliver as soon as possible.

In about a week everything was delivered and all of their stuff was placed in the home as Sarah did the arranging. They were now living in their new home. They had cancelled the leases on their apartments and closed out their utility bills and set up new service. Everything they ever wanted was in place including the success of the Partnership. John could throw away the package of condoms.

It was Saturday and time to look at the Bars for a possible purchase in two months. Tim met him at the first Bar and we asked a lot of questions to the owner What was the average revenue and what were the costs of doing business. The average revenue was $1000 or about a monthly take of $33,000. The cost of doing business including replenishing the liquor supply was about $10,000 or a net of $23,000. John asked at what price would he be willing to sell the Bar and the answer was $75,000, They thanked him and went to the 2nd Bar and asked the same questions. The bottom line was $65000.

Both Tim and John liked the first Bar better. They needed to know how much they were paying the Bar tenders and the number was a total of $3600 per month. They offered to buy the Bar at $65000. The owner countered at $70,000 if everything including the liquor supply was included.

Deal. The closing date would be in 60 days. John said his attorney would draw up the papers and John would name a Title Company to close the deal.

CHAPTER EIGHTY FIVE

John needed to call Paul Bass to draw up the papers for the purchases of the Bar. He gave Paul all the details and said the closing would be in two months. Did Paul send the document for the buyout of Maude and he said you should have it today. John thought that he and Maude go to the Bank he should also write a check to the bank to close out the loan. He would take two checks with him.

Jon needed to immediately send a memo to all the Limited Partners about what was going on so he wrote the following:

> Dear Limited Partners;
>
> One of the two General Partners passed away suddenly so that Partnership is now in the hands of his wife. I have decided to buy her out leaving only me as the General Partner. She has accepted $27,000 to attest that she longer has any relationship with the PHB partnership. That transaction will happen today or tomorrow.
>
> Secondly we will no longer accept any additional Limited Partners.
>
> Thirdly I will be paying off the loan of $60,000 that we took in order to buy the Pool Hall.

Fourthly the Partnership will make its first distribution to all the partners in about two months. Those who put in $10,000 will receive a distribution of $2500 AND those who put in $5000 will receive a distribution of $1250. The General Partner will receive a distribution of $10,000.

Fifthly the Partnership has purchased a Bar for $70,000. The transaction will close in 60 days.

Business continues to be good and the addition of the Bar will only enhance our business. Best wishes to all of you.

Sincerely,

John Drake
General Partner

Tim called to say that the FedEx package was there so he called Maude to meet him at the bank at 11Am. He picked up the FedEx package and two checks and headed to the Bank. He told the banker that he wanted to pay off the loan and what was total including any interest and the total was $60,600. He wrote a check for that amount and received a statement that the loan had been paid in full.

He also said that he had bought Dayton's wife's General Partnership and she would be here in a few minutes to accept a check for no longer had any relationship with the Partnership.

When she arrived John gave her the check and she signed the agreement.

When he got home that evening he printed the letter to the Limited Partners and would mail them tomorrow.

CHAPTER EIGHTY SIX

With the purchase of the Bar and the potential to purchase another Pool Hall in three months, John needed to consider quitting his job and finding an office space for himself. He talked to Sarah about it and she had mixed emotions She would be sorry to lose him as he had been a big help to herself and Judy. On the other hand the Partnership was growing and needed his full attention. They agreed that when the Bar purchase was closed in two months, he should resign. In the meantime John would look for place where he might lease office space.

Sarah's business has continued to flourish especially with opening accounts with a few of the Limited Partners and referrals. She has thought of leaving RBC and opening her own shop. If she did that, she would ask RBC to run the trades through them at a price. She would need to hire an assistant and find office space to determine what the expenses would be. She would be getting 100% of the commissions and, less the expenses, the net would be very attractive. In might be that she could share an office space with John with the proper space and security between the two businesses. There is a company Called Johnathon Cross that could accommodate her needs. She would discuss the situation with John. She felt that most of her big clients would follow her.

Things were a mess at their new home. They had cancelled their leases and mover all of her furniture etc to the new home. They spent a good deal of time situating all the furniture and other stuff and, slowly but surely, the place felt like home. They wanted to have a "house warming" so they picked a date and sent out invitations to about 40 people and began planning for that event. They decided to have the affair catered since neither one of them had the time to create the event. It would be costly but in the end worth the cost. The invitation specified that "no gifts were necessary".

In a few days John received the document from Paul regarding the purchase of the Bar. He called the owner and asked him to meet at his bank, RBC, at 11Am on Friday which he agreed to. He also set up a closing date with the same Title Company he had used before so they understood the drill. They would let the Seller and he know what that date would be. They met on Friday and signed and had notarized the document. John would write a check at the closing for $70,000.

CHAPTER EIGHTY SEVEN

The weekend was here and John and Sarah were happy as they needed to spend some time straightening out the house because the party would be next week on Sunday evening from 6 to 9PM. For the most part the house was in good shape so there wasn't much to do. They needed to go the store to buy some wine glasses and sturdy throw away plates and silverware and napkins. John decided to stop at the Pool Hall before shopping. Tim had just started on his shift so he had time to talk with John. The new Bar tender was doing well and the revenue was even doing better. He had to order more wine and beer which he charged to the PHB account. The Monday beer promotion continued to do well. John checked the mail and saw that there were some bills to be paid and he took care of them. Everyone seemed to be happy and were looking forward to coming to the house warming next week if they were able. He told Tim about the Bar he just purchased and would be buying another Pool Hall in the near future.

After leaving the Pool Hall he went directly to the part supply store and purchased what he needed. He added a few things to the list and went home. One of the things that were missing were indoor plants so they decided to go to the Nursery next Thursday night to purchase some plants.

They had two TVs which they could stream music from at the party. They located a good area that could be used for the wine and wine glasses. John called the liquor company the Pool Hall uses and ordered a case of a mixture of red and white wine plus soft drinks. He would get ice for the party on that Sunday afternoon.

They had been so busy with the house that they had not had a chance to relax. They decided to go out to dinner in the evening and picked Ontario's and made a reservation for 7PM. The meal would be costly but what the heck they could afford it.

It was 2PM and they didn't need to get ready to go out to eat for several hours so they decided to go shopping for two new outfits, one for each of them. Sarah purchased a stunning off the shoulder dress and John purchased a blue blazer and grey slacks off the rack plus a new pair of shoes.

CHAPTER EIGHTY EIGHT

Sunday was Church day and John has finally gotten Sarah to go with him to Church and Sunday School. She is really enjoying Sunday School and Church is just ok but she will continue to go. They usually go to the Deli after Church and will do so today. There is Hockey game at 1PM today and they have decided to make it to the game after lunch. They should have enough time. Both of them really enjoy the food at the deli and are always happy to go there. Maybe, they thought, they might try some place else. Sarah would get some suggestions from her associates for next Sunday but they probably would not go to Church because of the party Sunday evening.

On Monday John got a strange phone call at work. It was a man who gave his name as Richard Patrick as said he was a businessman in Windsor and would like to get to meet him someday for lunch. John said he only has 45 minutes for lunch on weekdays but it would work for Saturday. So they made a date to meet for lunch next Saturday at 11:30 at the Deli. John had no idea what this was all about except that it might just be a friendly get together. He would ask around about this guy but had no luck. He would just show up and see what happens.

He asked Sarah if she knew of him and she did not but would ask around. Sarah did find out that Mr. Patrick is the owner of several businesses in Windsor and that was all she found out. He would be there with an open mind.

John had gotten several phone calls in response to the letter he had sent about Dayton's death and the distribution. Most of the calls were very complimentary saying they hadn't expected to get any sort of distributions so soon and to keep up the good work. One guy was a bit upset that John was taking such a big distribution compared to the Limited Partners. John replied that is the was it works for General Partners as they do all the work and take the biggest risks. He seemed to be satisfied.

Instead of going to lunch a few days this week he poked around the area looking for a suitable place to office at. He was surprised that he found some really nice places in that business district and the rents seemed reasonable. He gave Sarah a short list of what he had found and asked her to check them out as possible choices for both of them. She said she would find the time to do that. If they found a suitable place that would accommodate both of them, hey saw no reason that they could not do it right away. She needed to talk to Johnathon Cross and see what the operation was like and if it suited her needs.

There was no Johnathon Cross in Windsor but there was a phone number in the States. She called the number and was switched to one of the Senior VIPs. They talked for about an hour and the bottom line was they would be very interested in discussing this further. They had several offices in Canada and the arrangement worked very well for all parties. They has a VP in Canada that was responsible for the offices in Canada. He would give Sarah's name and phone number to him and he would be in touch. Sarah was very encouraged by the phone call and shared the information with John.

Several days later the VP in Canada called Sarah and made an appointment to come to Windsor and meet with her next week. They decided on a place to meet where no one would see them and cause a problem for her with RBC.

CHAPTER EIGHTY NINE

Johnathon Cross had over 3,000 one man shops in North America mainly in the US. Richard Boulet was the VP from Johnathon Cross. His office was in Toronto. He spent over an hour explaining to Sarah how the system worked. They were a full service brokerage firm with all the necessary products. The system they have works very well in Canada as well as the US. It is very user friendly and delivers a much better compensation program than she currently has. In other words she would earn more money than what she is today. The company has an excellent reputation wherever they have offices. The system can easily be set up in a reasonable amount of time no matter where her office would be in Windsor.

The transfer of accounts can be handled with ease and you would find that your clients would be pleased with the promptness of the transfers. Since they have done this a thousand times it would be a piece of cake. They take great pride in the way they communicate with clients making them feel good about the transfer. It all sounded wonderful and would share the information with John this evening.

John was very much aware of Johnathon Cross in the US. They were very well regarded at home especially as a strong competitor to wire houses. Clients of Jones felt like they were getting more hands on care than they received at a wire house. The statements were easy to read and their executions were spot on. He did believe that Sarah would do extremely well working with Johnathon Cross. He thought it would be a great fit. If they worked in the same vicinity John could help out Sarah when he was not busy even just for answering her phone when she could not.

Sarah decided to go with Jones just as soon as she and John found a place to office at. Sarah would pay her share of the lease and the Partnership would pay its share. They continued to look in the same area that seemed friendly to businesses. They would select a large one room space with the option of putting up a divider to separate the two of them giving them good space and good security when a client comes to visit Sarah. Sarah thought for the time being she would try to get along without an assistant as John could help with the overflow of phone calls. She could always hire someone if the current system did not meet her needs.

They found the perfect office space that had a built in divider so they could function separately with ease. The rent was below what they thought they had to spend and it was available immediately. Sarah would need help in getting in touch with her clients. The best clients should could speak with them individually and the other contact by mail with the necessary transfer papers. It would be a struggle but John could help her. It would take several days for Johnathon Cross to set up her system and she could contact her clients in the meantime. Both she and John resigned their positions at RBC at the same time and the resignation went well for both parties.

Sarah had really good fortune getting 90% of her clients to switch. It took some struggling to get some to move but in the end it was almost perfect. She brought her computer with her and set up the Internet and phone with Bell Canada. Jones go the system set up in a short time so she was ready to go almost immediately with little down time.

John left the computer et al at the Pool Hall. He took a small file cabinet with him. He had his cell phone and didn't need a land line. He bought a computer and printer for the new office and had the Internet set up by Bell Canada. The ledger stayed at the Pool Hall. Amazing!. They were both set up without a hitch.

CHAPTER NINETY

It was Saturday and John had the 11AM appointment with Mr. Patrick at the Deli. John arrived a few minutes early dressed casually and found a vacant table and awaited Mr. Patrick. Pretty soon a rather large human being came into the Deli dressed in a suit and tie. He walked right over to John's table as if he knew John. John stood up and they shook hands.

Patrick started the conversation saying how glad he was to finally me him. He had heard good things about him through the grapevine. John said,meekly, how nice it was to meet a fellow business man. He went on to ask what kind of businesses he owned. Patrick smiled a bit and said a little bit of this and a little bit of that. He has lived in Windsor all of his life and knows a bunch of people in business in Windsor.

Patrick said I understand that you are a recent resident to Windsor and that you are an American. Is that true? Yes, matter of fact that is all true said John. What brought you to Windsor Mr. Drake? Please call me John he responded. I started a partnership with a good friend who I met in Dallas Texas. He was a long term resident in Windsor having played Hockey for a farm team of the Toronto Maple Leafs in Dallas.

What type of business did the partnership involve itself in? John said we owned a Pool Hall. My partner, Dayton Hudson, is recently deceased so I am the only General Partner at this time.

How interesting!. I too own a few Pool halls in Windsor. What a coincidence. What are your plans for the future? Are you planning to make other purchases in Windsor asked Mr. Patrick?

John said at this time he has no plans to purchase another Pool hall in Windsor. However, he has recently purchased a Bar here in Windsor.

Patrick responded by saying it is good news that you are not planning to purchase another Pool Hall here as it would be uncomfortable for you to be in completion with me.

A shot right between the eyes! John says thank you for that. I will take it under advisement. I don't think we have anything else to say to one another. Sorry, I have to go to another appointment said John and he gets up and leaves. Holy Cow! What a pronouncement!

CHAPTER NINETY ONE

Sarah, we may have a problem said John? I met with this guy Mr. Patrick who called me the other day saying he wanted to meet a fellow businessman so I took him up on the invitation having no idea as to his motive other than what he said. We exchanged chit chat and he asks me what kind of business I was in. When I told him that I owned a Pool Hall he wanted to know if I had plans to make other purchases. I said I just bought a bar. He said if I was planning to purchase another Pool Hall, it would be uncomfortable to be in competition with me. I said I needed to leave as I didn't think we had anything more to say to each other. What do you think?

It certainly looks like a threat to me. The way it could go is Canadian vs. American which could put a lot of pressure on your business said Sarah. You should wait a few months before you entertain the idea of buying another Pool Hall. In the meantime let's try and find out more about Mr. Patrick. We need to take a hard look at his holdings if we can. I do not know how to get that information. You need to call Paul to see if can find someone in Windsor that will have some information on Mr. Patrick. Be sure and tell him about the threat. He might have some good ideas.

John said he would call Paul today and go over the problem and quote what Patrick said to me. I left a message for him to call me, Is there a Better Business entity in Windsor? Look up the BBB on the computer which he did and found a link and a phone number. So he called them and set up an appointment to meet with them today at 11AM.

John met with them explaining the whole conversation with Peter McCoy who was the head guy at the BBB. Peter said that Mr. Patrick had sizeable holdings in Windsor which includes several Pool Halls. We have never had a complaint regarding any of his holdings, So from a business point of view he had a good reputation in Windsor. Peter went on to say to keep in touch with the him and he would look into the "threat" that he made to you. John thanked him very much and he thought he would continue on until he has a reason to call the BBB again.

After work on Thursday John and Sarah went to the neighborhood nursery to buy plants and flowers for the party on Sunday evening. It was getting close and they were excited about showing off their beautiful home. Other than setting things up on Saturday, there was nothing left to do.

CHAPTER NINETY TWO

It was Sunday and John and Sarah went through the house making sure everything was in its proper place. In the afternoon John would go to the sore to buy ice and put the white wine in a large bucket to chill. Sarah called the caterer to make sure everything was in the ready. They said they would begin setting up at 4PM.

At 6PM Sarah opened up the front door so people could just walk in. The response to the invitation was great and it seemed like everyone that was invited showed up. John and Sarah spent the evening chatting up the visitors. The party was hugely successful and John and Sarah were pleased. The food was wonderful and the servers did such a good job. John said that they could take a tax deduction for the cost of the party.

The last person left at 9:15 and so the cleanup would begin as they couldn't wait till Monday because it was a work day.

Sarah said she thought everyone had a good time and they got to meet folks they had never seen before especially limited partners. They didn't finish cleaning up until 11PM and they were tired and they went directly to bed.

When they awoke on Monday morning, they were excited to return to their brand new offices. The move was great no matter what you looked at. John was able to help Sarah with the phones as he was not busy much of the time. He was looking forward to the closing of the Bar purchase which was only a short time away. The extra revenue would really put them in good shape. They had about $100,000 balance and after the next two months they would have $226,000 but the cost of the Bar would reduce it to $156,000. After the next month the balance would be $242,000 and every month thereafter it would increase by $86,000. Perhaps in about two months we could consider buying another Pool Hall for about $100,000. He would even consider another distribution in the next quarter.

Sarah's business continues to improve to where she was earning about $100,000 a year with no stopping in sight. The family was doing very well.

CHAPTER NINETY THREE

John needed to have all mail including bills to come to his new office. Tell Tim when he orders next to tell the vendor to send all correspondence to John Drake at his new office. He would tell the Head Bar Tender to do the same. He would give each of them his new address. It will be John's responsibility to enter the invoices in the ledger book at the Pool Hall and the ledger book at the Bar when John takes.

Position. He would purchase the new ledger book in the next two weeks and eventually tell George, the Head Bar Tender and the 2nd shift barkeep, about the ledger.

John called Tim on the phone to ask him if he knows Patrick, and if so, what kind of person is he. Tim said Patrick is a big deal in Windsor as he owns a bunch of properties including several Pool Halls. You do not want to mess with him. His tentacles stretch out far in Windsor. John said if he calls you will you let me know and Tim said of course.

Pete, John's brother called, to tell him that he was getting married in a month. Could he make it to the wedding and John declined but wished him good luck. Things were going well for John and Sarah and was sorry they could not come to the wedding. Sarah just left RBC to go with Johnathon Cross and he was sharing an office with her. He had quit his job at RBC also because the Partnership was requiring much attention.

After talking with Pete he called his parents as he had not talked to them in over a month. Since they were Limited Partners they would have received the memo that John sent regarding all that was going on in Windsor. He did tell them about both he and Sarah quitting their jobs at RBC and Sarah joining Johnathon Cross opening her own office in Windsor. John was sharing that office with her. He needed to quit his job because the Partnership was requiring much of his time. Maybe they could make a trip to visit he and Sarah in Windsor in the spring.

Tim called John to tell him that Mr. Patrick called him and offered him a job at one of his Pool Halls at more money than John was Paying him. That salary would be $3000 per month. John said he would match that salary as Tim was too valuable to lose and Tim accepted the offer. Wow. That was a close one. This guy Patrick means business.

After he got off the phone with Tim, he told Sarah what happened and she was 100% in agreement with what John did. How are we going to contend with this guy who will continue, no doubt, to rattle their cage.

John called Mr. McCoy at the BBB and told him that Patrick was trying to hire one of his top employees away from him by offering him more money. John did not have an option so he met Patrick's offer. What can he do to stop him? McCoy said he would think it over and get back to him.

CHAPTER NINETY FOUR

Since it was only a few days before the closing for the Barr, John went to Barnes and Noble to purchase a ledger book. After the purchase he went to the Bar to show George how to use it and about bringing the cash to the Bank after the close, He also asked George if he knows Mr. Patrick and George said he did. What can you tell me about him says John. George responded by saying that he was a very big deal in Windsor owning a number of Pool Halls and perhaps even Bars. John asked George to let him know if Mr. Patrick contacts him.

John got a call from Mr. McCoy regarding Mr. Patrick. He said that he told Mr. Patrick that if he continues to harass you the BBB will lower his rating. He hoped that would help John. John was thankful that McCoy was pro active in the matter and yet he was still concerned that Patrick would continue to be a pain in his ass. What then?

John decided to talk to the other Pool Hall that was in the final two choices when they bought "Dayton Hudson". The owner said he would still liked to sell the Hall at $95,000. John said he would get back to him just as soon as he was ready to strike a deal. Sarah was a bit wary of the conversation John had with the Pool Hall owner,

He contacted Paul to see if he was able to get any information on Mr. Patrick. Paul said the only information he got was that Patrick was a major investor in Pool Halls and Bars. John told Paul about the conversation he had with the BBB and Paul said that it was a step in the right direction. That afternoon he got a call from Mr. Patrick asking for another meeting which John agreed to. They were to meet at the Deli in two days at 11AM. Was he taking a risk in going to this meeting? John figured he had nothing to lose.

The meeting took place on Thursday. Patrick seemed very cordial which surprised John. Mr. Patrick said that he wanted to stop harassing John and had a proposal to make. If John would take on Patrick as a General Partner, he would put his best Pool Hall and best Bar in the Partnership. John was completely blind sided by the offer. Certainly he would consider the proposal, They shook hands on went on their ways./

Could Patrick be trusted? He needed to get opinions from others especially Sarah and Tim. Sarah's first thought was no way but the more she thought about it she said John should ask for an infusion of cash in addition to the Pool Hall and Bar. John thought it was a good idea. Perhaps the $30,000 that John and Dayton had put in initially. Tim was very positive about the offer. Paul said the addition of $20,000 would be a good deal.

John called Patrick requesting another meeting on next Monday at 11Am at the Deli. The meeting took place and John made the proposal to Mr. Patrick. He also said that in the agreement nether of the Partners could take out money without the other Partner's approval. Patrick said give him a few days to consider the offer. He also told Patrick that John would toe point man in the Partnership being directly responsible for the day to day running of the properties.

John called Paul and asked him to draft a document with Mr. Patrick as they additional General Partner with the caveat that no money could be withdrawn without both partners agreeing. The language would be the same as the agreement that he and Dayton had agreed to with the one addition being the $20,000 cash infusion.

CHAPTER NINETY FIVE

Sarah had a big announcement to make to John. She was pregnant 6 weeks along which means birth in 7 ½ months. John was ecstatic over the news. Is it a boy or girl asked John. Too soon to tell but I am not sure I want to know said Sarah. I want it to be a surprise. That was ok with John.

They needed to find a live in Nanny soon. Sarah only wants to take a few days off after the birth and go back to work, John approved. Sarah also announced that she wanted to breast feed the baby. John had no comment. Since Sarah's parents live close by, her Mom could be a big help also.

John asked when do we setup the nursery for the baby. Too soon said Sarah. Maybe in about 5 months. He needed to tell his parents and his brother. He would call them tonight,

Richard Patrick called on Thursday. He said he approved all the conditions of the Partnership and was ready to sign the paperwork. John told him that his attorney was drawing up the papers and it would be ready in a few days. In the meantime John called Paul to give him further details of the deal which included a Pool Hall, a Bar and $20,000 in cash. Paul said it would be in the mail in a few days.

John asked Richard what was the average monthly revenue for the Pool Hall and the Bar. In addition John needed to know the expenses including the salaries of all the employees, the rent and utility bills, What was the average cost of liquor and beer? He also needed to know the names and responsibility of each of the employees.

At the get go John needs to talk to all the employees about the ledger book which lists all the costs of doing business and the daily take. The money will need to be taken to the Partnership's Bank by the 2nd shift bar tender.

Richard was amazed at how detailed the operation would be. As far as the rent he owned the buildings so the rent would be paid to him. I will go over the list of employees and the expenses after the deal has been done while waiting for the closing of the properties. So basically I don't have any responsibility in the Partnership except any additional properties would be discussed in addition to any distributions. I need to have a regular weekly meeting with you to discuss any concerns, problems and the such.

John was ok with all those details and looking forward to a healthy and profitable relationship. When the document shows up, you need to meet me at our Bank to have it notarized and to meet our Banker. Also it would be helpful if I knew what other businesses you own as that list might come in handy one day. Richard would give him that information at the closing. By the way who is your Banker. John said John Riley at RBC. Richard knows him well.

CHAPTER NINETY SIX

He forgot to tell Paul about his new office address which he is sharing with Sarah who has left RBC and joined Johnathon Cross. Please send all correspondence t that new address. Phone number is the same. You need to take a trip here one of these days.

John has second thoughts about Richard Patrick but, then again, the deal was a good one. The cash flow would be great and he would be running the show for the most part. He can't wait until he gets the information from John about the revenue. Two Pool Halls and two Bars would be their portfolio.

The closing would be in 10 days and it can't be done earlier. The Title Company has to check the taxes and liens on the property. He would call the Title to see if they could move the closing up a week. The Title Company said they could do that so he called Richard to give him the new closing date. Richard needed to get all the information together that John requested so he could be ready for the closing.

John needed to go to the store to buy two ledger books for the new Pool Hall and Bar. He did not think that the transition would be difficult. He would still have control of the check book and all bills would come through him. He did, however, have lots to do after the closing.

He called Paul to se if the document regarding the new General Partner was ready. Paul said it was going by FedEx today to John's new address. The agreement was pretty cut and dried. Mr. Patrick should have no trouble in signing. Jon needs to make several copies of the agreement one to Richard and one to his Banker. Mr. Riley and one for him. It should be very interesting seeing what holdings Richard had in addition to the Pool Hall and the Bar he was putting in the partnership. Richard reasoning to agree to the deal was he thought John could do a better job of marketing and managing the properties than he could. Richard needs to focus on his other properties.

CHAPTER NINETY SEVEN

John heard from the Title Company that there was lien on the two properties of $22,000. Until that lien is met the deal cannot go through. John called Richard and told him the deal cannot work until the lien is met which was $22,000. Either he picks two other properties that are free and clear or pays off the lien, the deal is dead. Richard said to give him a day or two to decide.

Don't count your chickens until they are hatched is what John told himself. Maybe it will still work. Sarah said Patrick knew about the money owed on those two properties. What did he think was going to happen when you found out about the lien? Of course, you would not agree with the deal. I do not trust him. If he comes back with two different properties, you need to know what the revenue is for those properties.

John called again and asked him to provide the monthly revenue minus expenses on the new properties if that is the direction he wants to go. That is ok with Richard. So John has to wait for Richard's decision.

A few days later Richard calls and says he will put up the $22,000 to void the lien in the next few days. John was pleased with the decision so the closing can proceed on the appointed day. The Title Company called the next day and said the closing can continue on the appointed day as Mr. Patrick has satisfied the lien.

On the day of the closing, Richard gave John a list of all the businesses he owned and the revenue minus expenses for the Pool Hall and Bar. The breakdown is as follows:

Two pool halls
One bar
One office cleaning business
One home cleaning company
Two movie theatres
Two restaurants
One drug store
One plant nursery
The closing went well and John got the information he needed
The monthly net for the new Pool Hall is $60,000
The monthly net for the new Bar is $23,000

So the total net for the two Pool halls and the two Bars is $169,000. The total balance after one month of all the properties is $114,000 plus $169,00 or a grand total of $283,000. A distribution is called: General Partners will receive $20,000 each, The $10.000 purchasers will get $5000. Each of the Limited Partners who purchased $5000 will receive $2500 The total distributions is $164,000. This distributions will occur in about 30 days. The balance at that time after the distribution is $119,000

     PHILIP STEPHENS

CHAPTER NINETY EIGHT

The letter will go out as follows;

Dear Partners

I am pleased to announce the addition of a new General Partner, Richard Patrick immediately. I am also pleased to announce the acquisition of one more pool hall and one more bar making the total of two of each without any cost plus the addition of $20,000 to the balance.

The letter will read as follows;

I am pleased to announce a new General Partner, Richard Patrick. I am also pleased to announce the addition of one Pool Hall plus one Bar. The total balance is $114,000 plus $86,000 or a total of $200000 At the end of next month the balance will be about $363,000

I am also announcing a distribution to all partners in about 30 days:

General Partners will get $20,000 each

Limited Partners who purchased a $10,000 interest will receive $5000.

Limited Partners who purchased a $5000 interest will receive $2500

The total distribution is $165,000 leaving a balance of $198,000

The projected balance in two months will be about $361,000. I project another distribution in about two to three months.

Richard will be surprised that he will be getting a $20,000 distribution in a month which will return to him the amount he put up to begin with. John needs to talk with Richard about the possibility of purchasing another Pool Hall or Bar in three months. I gave him the projected balance in two months to be $361,000 and 3 months to be $424,000. There will be another distribution during that period which would amount to $185,000 leaving $239,000. Richard attitude was great for all the Partners. Lets wait until the next two months go by and see where we are at that time. John agreed.

So as we leave John and Sarah, she is happy in her new office and John is doing much better than expected. Richard is not a threat anymore and is happy as a pig in mud. Soon there will be an addition to the family leading to more happiness for Sarah and John.